Cardula and the LOCKED ROOMS

By Jack Ritchie

Introduction by Brian Skupin

Cardula and the LOCKED ROOMS

By Jack Ritchie
Introduction by Brian Skupin

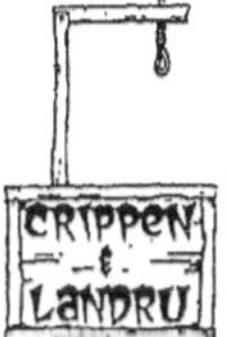

CRIPPEN & LANDRU PUBLISHERS
Cincinnati, Ohio
2026

For information contact:
Crippen & Landru, Publishers
P. O. Box 532057
Cincinnati, OH 45253 USA

Web: www.crippenlandru.com
E-mail: Info@crippenlandru.com

ISBN (softcover): 978-1-971489-00-1
ISBN (clothbound): 978-1-971489-01-8

First Edition: January 2026
10 9 8 7 6 5 4 3 2 1

Contents

Introduction to Cardula
and the Locked Rooms

"The short story seems to be my field, possibly by forfeit."
--Jack Ritchie

Jack Ritchie was one of the last mystery writers to earn his living entirely by short stories, and by the time of his death was one of the most successful short story writers in crime fiction history. The hallmarks of a Ritchie story are ingenious twists on classic situations, a wry humor, often at the expense of the narrator, and an extraordinary economy of style.

Ritchie's ability to turn out efficient stories is legendary. Elliot Roosevelt said "He can do more in a few thousand words than most writers can manage in a trilogy." Francis M. Nevins, Jr. called him "one of the finest writers of short mysteries (and I do mean short) that ever breathed." Bill Pronzini said Ritchie has "an amazing ability to put more plot and more characterization into fewer words than any crime writer past or present." And in a much-quoted observation, Anthony Boucher said "No word is wasted, and many words serve more than one purpose… Ritchie can write a long short story that is virtually the equivalent of a full suspense novel; and his very short stories sparkle as lapidary art."

But the best description of Ritchie's concision came from the man himself:

> "I've always felt that there hasn't been a novel published that couldn't be reduced to a better short story… Victor Hugo put about 30,000 words into *Les Misérables* delineating the history, structure, and whatnot of the Paris sewers. Now if I'd been in his shoes I could have described the sewers in two paragraphs. Maybe one. Les *Misérables* itself would have become a novelette. Possibly even a pamphlet."

Jack Ritchie was born in 1922 as John George Reitci, the son of Hungarian immigrants to the USA. His father, Joseph, was a tailor, and his mother Irma (Bielohratzky), a homemaker. After an uneventful childhood and graduation from Boys' Technical High School in Milwaukee, he spent two years in Teachers' College at what is now the University of Wisconsin—Milwaukee. He was drafted into the United States Army in 1942 and served as a Private, where, he reported, he "cried for three years, three months, and twenty-one days."

After the war, Ritchie returned to his parents' home and tried to go to college again, using the financial benefits of the G.I. Bill, but it didn't work out, so he worked for several years in his father's tailor shop.

His mother Irma was an active member of the Milwaukee Amateur Press Club (President in 1954 and Executive Chairman in 1955) and an aspiring fiction writer. Through her Ritchie met Lawrence (Larry) Sternig, a literary agent, and had his first (non-mystery) story published in *The New York Daily News* in 1953. He was married shortly thereafter, to another writer, Rita Krohne, with whom he would eventually have four children. Ritchie's native wit can be seen in the comment he made about having to hold the wedding reception in his parents' small house: he claimed to have divided the guests into two groups and given them instructions such that "while one half inhaled, the other half exhaled!"

For the next several years Ritchie wrote stories for publications including *Good Housekeeping, Manhunt, Boy's Life*, and *Zane Grey Western Magazine*, and the stories were as diverse as the periodicals. In "The Chesterfield" what appears to be a simple procedural story about a cop investigating a missing person turns into a creepy horror story. "#8" is a taut tale of the meeting of a serial killer and victim. For *Boy's Life* he wrote a series about exchange students from Lichtenstein coming to play sports in the USA.

Alfred Hitchcock's Mystery Magazine was founded in 1956, and while Ritchie continued writing and selling across genres, this quickly became his major market. In the 1950's and 1960's Ritchie's agent also sold story rights to several of the newly popular television anthology series, including *The Unforeseen, Tales of the Unexpected*, and *Alfred Hitchcock Presents*.

Ritchie became an anthologist's favorite. Stories such as "Shatterproof," about a man who tries to persuade the hitman his wife hired not to kill him; "For All the Rude People," about how a man chooses to spend his time when he finds out he is dying; and "The Green Heart," about a man who schemes to marry a rich woman for her money, all appeared in multiple collections. And he became a regular resident in the annual *Best Mysteries of the Year* collections published by Dutton, eventually superseding Ellery Queen for first place in total number of appearances.

Rita Ritchie's career, as a writer for children and teenagers, was also successful. Her books were twice selected by the Junior Literary Guild; she wrote several of the popular Big Little Books, and some short stories. She and Jack were active on the Wisconsin literary scene, and both won Short Fiction awards from the Council of Wisconsin Writers. In the acknowledgments to her 1961 novel, *The Enemy at the Gate* (Dutton), Rita wrote, "Not the least of my gratitude goes to Jack Ritchie, the kind and understanding spouse who each day mercilessly drove me to my typewriter."

Later in life, Jack and Rita would divorce, but they had what must have been one of the best nights of their lives in the spring of 1971. According to the April 8 edition of The *Milwaukee Journal* the two attended the premiere of the Elaine May—Walter Matthau movie, *A New Leaf,* based on Ritchie's story "The Green Heart." The paper stated that Ritchie received $20,000 for the rights, and continued:

> "It was an exciting premiere for them both as they watched Jack's story come to life on the screen. Then they continued to the Wisconsin Club where they hobnobbed with other writers and where, after dinner, Rita was awarded the $500 prize for having written the year's best juvenile book, Night Coach to Paris. About midnight the Cinderella couple took their coach back to their Fort Atkinson farm."

"The Green Heart" was also adapted into a musical which played in 1997 at New York's Variety Arts Theater.

Despite his tremendous success, Ritchie mentioned an ongoing frustration in a 1972 interview: "I've never been able to sell to *Ellery Queen Mystery Magazine*, despite some thirty to forty submissions." This situation was resolved in 1976, when "Nobody Tells Me Anything" appeared. It was nominated for the Edgar award for Best Short Story from the Mystery Writers of America (MWA), as were two later *EQMM* stories. In 1981 Ritchie's story "The Absence of Emily" won the Edgar.

After writing standalone stories for years, Ritchie finally started two series: one about police detective Henry Turnbuckle, and one about an unusual private investigator: Cardula.

Henry is often too clever for his own good, who analyzes and over-analyzes each case, sometimes with the knowing and bemused assistance of his deadpan partner, Ralph. Whether Henry solves the case or not, by the end of the story he is frequently on his way to enjoying a glass of sherry with a violet-eyed, auburn-haired woman. "Box in a Box" is a perfect introduction to Henry and is included here. The entire series was collected in *The Adventures of Henry Turnbuckle* (Southern Illinois University Press, 1987), edited with an outstanding introduction by Francis M. Nevins, Jr.

Ritchie's Cardula stories have never been collected before, and all nine are included here. One of the many charms of these stories is that

Ritchie never explicitly states the unusual nature of his main character (neither will I), instead sprinkling a few subtle, and not so subtle, clues throughout the tales. Just when the reader forgets that the narrator is anything special, in comes another unexpected and humorous reminder. The first in the series, "Kid Cardula," appeared in the June 1976 issue of *Alfred Hitchcock's Mystery Magazine*, and features Cardula, needing money, taking advantage of his unusual strength to win boxing purses.

It wasn't apparent that Cardula would be a series character, or an occasional private investigator, until the second story, "The Cardula Detective Agency." Cardula's unusual attributes provide significant advantages in his work as a P.I., and through this work he is able to make a living, so to speak. It's with this story that the bizarre situations common to much of Ritchie's work appear in the Cardula series. In "The Canvas Caper" a man has been tasked with murdering a blackmailer but instead tries to get Cardula to do it, with unexpected results. "Cardula to the Rescue" sees him intervene in a purse-snatching and be reproofed for it by the owner of the purse, after which he discovers a plot, counter-plot, and counter-counter plot. In "Cardula and the Kleptomaniac" Cardula is asked to discover who has been, for years, stealing worthless trinkets from friends. "Cardula's Revenge" addresses Cardula's past and shows him cleverly outmaneuvering an old antagonist. Although most of the stories are notable for their ingenuity and feature detection, "The Return of Cardula" stands out as a story that could have been written by Ellery Queen, with its baseball milieu and dying message. "Cardula and the Locked Rooms" sees Cardula hired to confirm who stole a valuable painting by someone who had previously stolen the same painting. And in 1983's "Cardula and the Briefcase," the last in the series, Cardula is asked to solve the murder of a burglar's partner, and ends up solving an entirely different case.

"The Return of Cardula," with its baseball milieu and wordplay solution, could have been an Ellery Queen tale.

Despite writing "Cardula and the Locked Rooms" Ritchie was not known for the locked room mystery. But six of his stories qualify as locked rooms--or the more general "impossible crimes"--while still retaining his usual mix of wit and irony, and they are all included here. "Box in a Box" pits Henry Turnbuckle's unstoppable analysis against a classic locked room mystery, and reminds one of the paradoxical "anyone could have done it" approach Christianna Brand used in her best impossible stories. "Pearls Before Wine" is about a perplexingly swift theft of pearls at a party. "The Crime Machine" is one of Ritchie's best and most complex stories, and has two impossibilities. "Swing High" is an efficient procedural about an insurance investigation until it suddenly goes in a different direction, and as a bonus has a unique solution to the impossible defenestration problem. "Upside Down World" features an insurance investigator investigating an apparent death by heart attack, and has one of the most credible methods of causing a "natural" death that I've seen. "Play a Game of Cyanide" starts with what I consider Ritchie's best opening line, and follows the attempts of an investigator to find poison that remains hidden despite an exhaustive search—another Ellery Queen trademark.

Late in life, Ritchie did complete an adventure novel, *Tiger Island* (First Class, 1987), which was published posthumously. But his entire career was based on short stories. He wrote hundreds of mystery short stories; won the MWA's highest short story award, had them adapted to television, film, and the stage, and was recognized by his anthologists and peers. There may be no quote about him more apt than this epitaph by Bill Pronzini.

"For more than 30 years, Jack Ritchie was one of the two or three best writers of the criminous short story."

Brian Skupin
New York, New York

July, 2025

Sources

"Introduction," *Perfect Crimes*, Elliott Roosevelt, St. Martin's Press, 1989

"Introduction," Francis M. Nevins, Jr., *Better Mousetraps,* St. Martin's Press, 1988

Tricks and Treats, Ed. by Joe Gores and Bill Pronzini, p. 229, Doubleday Crime Club, 1976

"Introduction," Donald Westlake, *A New Leaf,* Dell, 1971

"Jack Ritchie: An Interview," Ray Puechner, *The Armchair Detective*, Volume 6, Number 1, October 1972,

Chatterbox, Irma Reitci, Volume VI, October 1954, United Amateur Press Association

"Introduction," Francis M. Nevins, Jr., *Little Boxes of Bewilderment,* St. Martin's Press, 1989

The Murder Mystique, Lucy Freeman, Ungar, 1982

Cardula

Kid Cardula

It's just about time for me to close down the gym for the night when this tall stranger comes up to me.

He wears a black hat, black suit, black shoes, black topcoat, and he carries a zipper bag.

His eyes are black, too. "I understand that you manage boxers?"

I shrug. "I had a few good boys in my time."

Sure, I had few good boys, but never *real* good. The best I ever done was with Chappie Strauss. He was listed as number ten in the lightweight division by *Ring Magazine*. Once. And I had to pick my fights careful to get him that far. Then he meets Galanio, which is a catastrophe, and he loses his next four fights too before I decide it's time to retire him.

"I would like you to manage me," the stranger says. "I plan to enter the fight ring."

I look him over. He seems well built and I put his weight at around one-ninety. Height maybe six foot one. But he looks pale, like his face hasn't seen the sun for some time. And there is also the question of his age. It's hard to pin-point, but he's no kid.

"How old are you?" I ask.

He shifts a little. "What is the ideal age for a boxer?"

"Mister," I say, "in this state it's illegal for any man over forty to even step into the ring."

"I'm thirty," he says fast. "I'll see to it that you get a birth certificate to verify that."

I smiled a little. "Look, man, at thirty in this game, you're just about over the hill. Not starting."

His eyes glitter a little. "But I am strong. Incredibly strong."

I stretch the smile to a grin. "Like the poet says, you got the strength of ten because your heart is pure?"

He nods. "I do have the strength of ten, though not for that reason. As a matter of fact, realizing that I possessed this tremendous strength, it finally occurred to me that I might as well capitalize on it. Legitimately."

He puts down the zipper bag and walks over to where a set of barbells is laying on the mat and does a fast clean and jerk like he was handling a baby's rattle.

I don t know how many pounds is on that bar, weightlifting not being my field. But I remember seeing Wisniewski working with those weights a couple of hours ago and he grunts and sweats and Wisniewski is a heavyweight with a couple of state lifting titles to his credit.

I'm a little impressed, but still not interested. "So you're strong. Maybe I can give you the names of a few of the weightmen who work out here. They got some kind of a club."

He glares, at which he seems good. "There is no money in weight lifting and I need a great deal of money." He sighs. "The subject of money never really entered my mind until recently. I simply dipped into my capital when necessary and then suddenly I woke one evening to discover that I was broke."

I look him over again. His clothes look expensive, but a touch shabby, like they been worn too long and maybe slept in.

"I do read the newspapers," he says, "including the sports pages, and I see that there is a fortune to be made in the prize ring with a minimum of effort." He indicates the zipper bag. "Before I ran completely out of money, I bought boxing trunks and shoes. I will have to borrow the boxing gloves."

I raise an eyebrow. 'You mean you want to step into the ring with somebody right now?"

"Precisely."

I look down the gym floor. By now the place is empty except for Alfie Bogan who's still working out on the heavy bag.

Alfie Bogan is a good kid and a hard worker. He's got a fair punch and high hopes for the ring. So far he's won all six of his fights, three by knockouts and three by decisions. But I can't see what's in his future. He just don't have enough to get to the top.

All right, I think to myself. Why not give the gentleman in black a tryout and get this over with so I can get to bed, which is a cot in my office.

I call Alfie over and say, "This here nice man wants to step into the ring with you for a couple of rounds."

It's O.K. with Alfie so the stranger disappears into the locker room and comes back wearing black trunks.

I fit him gloves, and he and Alfie climb into the ring and go to opposite corners.

I take the wrapper off a new cigar, strike the gong, and start lighting up.

Alfie comes charging out of his corner, the way he always does, and meets the stranger three-quarters of the way across the ring. He throws a right and a left hook, which the stranger shrugs off. Then the stranger flicks out his left. You don't really see it, you just know it happened. It connects with Alfie's chin and Alfie hits the canvas on his back and stays there. I mean he's out.

I notice that my match is burning my fingers and quick blow it out. Then I climb into the ring to look at Alfie. He's still breathing, but he won't be awake for a while.

When you been in the fight game as long as I have, you don't need no long study to rate a fighter. Just that one left—and even the sound of it connecting—has got my heart beating a little faster.

I look around the gym for somebody to replace Alfie, but like I said before, it's empty. I lick my lips. "Kid, what about your right hand? Is it anywhere near as good as your left?"

"Actually my right hand is the better of the two."

I begin to sweat with the possibilities. "Kid, I'm impressed with your punch. I admit that. But the fight game is more than just punching. Can you take a punch too?"

He smiles thin like a kid wearing new braces. "Of course. Please hit me."

Why not? I think. I might as well find out right now if he can take a punch. I take the glove off Alfie's right hand and slip into it.

In my day which was thirty years ago—I had a pretty good right and I think I still got most of it. So I haul off and give it all I got. Right on the button of his chin.

And then I hop around the ring with tears in my eyes because I think I just busted my hand, but the stranger is still standing there with that narrow smile on his face and his hair not even mussed.

Alfie comes back into this world while I'm checking my hand and am relieved to discover that it ain't broken after all.

He groans and staggers to his feet, ready to start all over again. "A lucky punch." The boy is all heart, but no brains.

"No more tonight, Alfie," I say. "Some other time."

I send him off to the showers and take the stranger into my office. 'What's your name?"

"I am known as Cardula."

Cardula? Probably Puerto Rican, I guess. He's got a little accent.

"All right," I say, "from now on you're Kid Cardula. Call me Manny."

I light my cigar. "Kid, I just may be able to make something out of you. But first, let's get off on the right foot by making everything legal. First thing tomorrow morning we see my lawyer and he'll draw papers which make us business associates."

Kid Cardula looks uneasy. "Unfortunately I can't make it tomorrow morning. Or the afternoon. For that matter, I can't make it any morning or afternoon."

I frown. "Why not?"

"I suffer from what may be termed photophobia."

"What the hell is photophobia?"

"I simply cannot endure sunlight."

"You break out in a rash or something?"

"Quite a bit more than a rash."

I chew my cigar. "Does this photophobia hurt your fighting any?"

"Not at all. Actually I regard it as responsible for my strength. However, all of my matches will have to be scheduled for evenings."

"Not much sweat there. Damn near all matches today are in the evening anyway." I think a little while. "Kid, I don't think we need to mention this photophobia to the State Medical Commission. I don't know how they stand on the subject and it's better we take no chances. This photophobia isn't catching, is it?"

"Not in the usual sense." He smiles wide this time, and I see why he's been smiling tight before. He's got these two outsize upper teeth, one on each side of his mouth. Personally, if I had teeth like that, I'd have them pulled, whether they got cavities or not.

He clears his throat. "Manny, would it be at all possible for me get an advance on my future earnings?

Ordinarily if anybody I just meet for the first time asks me for money I tell him to go to hell. But with Kid Cardula and his future, I think I can make an exception. "Sure, Kid," I say. "I guess you're a little short on eating money?"

"I am not particularly concerned about eating money," the Kid says. "But my landlord threatens to evict me if I don't pay the rent."

The morning at around eleven I get a phone call from Hanahan. It's about the McCardle-Jabloncic main event on Saturday night's card at the arena.

McCardle is Hanahan's pride and joy. He's a heavyweight, got some style and speed, and he's young. Hanahan is bringing him along carefully, picking and choosing. Maybe McCardle isn't exactly championship material, but he should get in a few big money fights before it's time to retire.

"Manny," Hanahan says, "we got a little trouble with the Saturday night card. Jabloncic showed up at the weigh-ins with a virus, so he got scratched. I need somebody to fill in. You got anybody around there who'll fill the role?"

Jabloncic has eighteen wins and ten losses, which record don't look too bad on paper, except that it don't mention that he got six of them losses—all by knockouts—in a row after his eighteenth win. So I know exactly what type of fighter Hanahan wants as a substitute for Jabloncic.

I think a little. Off hand, there are three or four veterans who hang around the gym and could use the money and don't mind the beating.

And then I remember Kid Cardula.

Ordinarily when you got a new boy, you bring him up slow, like three-round preliminaries. But with Kid Cardula I feel I got something that can't wait and we might as well take some shortcuts.

I speak into the phone. "Well, off hand, Hanahan, I can't think of anybody except this new face that just come to me last night. Kid Cardula, I think he calls himself."

"Never heard of him. What's his win-lose?"

"I don't know. He's some kind of foreign fighter. Puerto Rico, I think. I don't have his records yet."

Hanahan is cautious. "You ever seen him fight?

"Well, I put him in the ring here for just a few seconds to see if he has anything. His left is fair, but I never seen him use his right hand once. Don't even know if he has one."

Hanahan is interested. "Anything else?"

"He came in here wearing a shabby suit and gave me a sob story about being down and out. He's thirty-five if he's a day. I'll swear to that."

Hanahan is pleased. "Well, all right. But I don't want anybody too easy. Can he stand up for a couple of rounds?"

"Hanahan, I can't guarantee anything, but I'll try the best I can."

That evening, when Kid Cardula shows up at the gym, I quick rush him to my lawyer and then to the weigh-in and physical under the arena, where I also sign papers which gives us ten percent of the night's gross.

I provide Kid Cardula with a robe which has got no lettering on it yet, but it's black, his favorite color, and we go out into the arena. McCardle is a local boy, which means he's got a following. Half the neighborhood is at the arena and it ain't really a bad house. Not like the old days, but good enough.

We set up shop inside the ring and when the bell rings, McCardle makes the sign of the cross and dances out of his corner.

But Kid Cardula don't move an inch. He turns to me, and he looks scared. "Does McCardle have to do that?"

"Do what?" I ask. "Now look, Kid, this is no time to get stage fright Get out there and fight."

The Kid peeks back over his shoulder where the referee and McCardle are waiting for him in the center of the ring. Then he takes a deep breath, turns, and glides out of our corner.

His left whips out, makes the connection with McCardle's jaw, and it's all over. Just like that. McCardle is lying there in the same pose as Alfie Bogan last night.

Even the referee is stunned and wastes a few seconds getting around to the count, not that it really matters. The bout is wrapped up in nineteen seconds, including the count.

There's some booing. Not because anybody thinks that McCardle threw the fight, but because everything went so quick with the wrong man winning and the fans figure they didn't get enough time for the price of their tickets.

When we're back in the dressing room, the first person who comes storming in is Hanahan, his face beet red. He glares at Kid Cardula and then drags me to a corner. "What the hell are you doing to me, Manny?"

I am all innocence. "Hanahan, I swear that was the luckiest punch."

"You're damn right it was a lucky punch. We'll have the rematch as soon as I can book the arena again."

"Re-match?" I rub my chin. "Maybe so, Hanahan, but in truth, I feel that I got to protect the Kid's interests. It's like a sacred trust. So for the rematch, we make his cut of the gate sixty percent instead of ten, right?

Hanahan is fit to explode, but he's got this black spot on his fighter's record and the sooner he gets it off, the better. So by the time we finish yelling at each other, we decide to split the purse fifty-fifty, which's about what I expect anyway.

A couple of nights later when I close up the gym and go to my office, I find the Kid sitting there watching the late show on my portable TV set. It's one of them Dracula pictures and he turns to another channel when I enter.

I nod. "Never could stand them vampire pictures myself either. Even in a movie, I like logic, and they ain't got no logic."

"No logic?"

"Right. Like when you start off with one vampire and he goes out and drinks somebody's blood and that turns his victim into a vampire too, right? So now there's two vampires. A week later, they both get hungry and go out and feed on two victims. Now you got *four* vampires.

A week later them four vampires go out to feed and now you got eight vampires."

"Ah, yes," Kid Cardula says. "And at the end of twenty-one weeks, one would logically expect to have a total of 1,048,576 vampires?"

"About that. And at the end of thirty weeks or so, everybody on the face of the earth is a vampire, and a week later all of them starve to death because they got no food supply any more."

Kid Cardula smiles, showing them big teeth. "You've got a head on your shoulders, Manny. However, suppose that these fictitious vampires, realizing that draining all of the blood from their victims will turn them into vampires and thereby competitors, exercise a certain restraint instead? Suppose they simply take a sip, so to speak, from one person and a sip from the next, leaving their victims with just a slight anemia and lassitude for a few days, but otherwise none the worse for wear?"

I nod, turn down the TV volume, and get back to the fight business.

"Now, Kid, I know that you'll be able to put McCardle away again in a few seconds, but we got to remember that fighting is also show biz. People don't pay good money for long to see twenty-second fights. We got to give the customers a performance that lasts awhile. So when we get McCardle again, I want you to carry him for a few rounds. Don't hit too hard. Make the match look even until say the fifth round and then put him away."

I light a cigar. "If we look too good, Kid, we'll have trouble getting opponents later and we got to think about the future. A string of knockouts is fine, Kid, but don't make them look too easy."

In the weeks which follow while we're waiting for the McCardle rematch, I can't get the Kid to do any training at all—no road work and he won't even consider shadow boxing in front of a mirror.

So I leave it at that, not wanting to tamper with something that might be perfect. Also he won't give me his address. I suppose he's just got pride and don't want me to see the dump in which he lives. And he's got no phone. But he shows up at the gym every other night or so just in case there's something concerning him.

The second McCardle fight comes, and we take it in stride. The Kid carries McCardle for four rounds, but still making the bouts look good and then in the fifth round he puts McCardle away with a short fast right.

In the days which follow, we don't have any particular trouble signing up more fights because we'll take any bout which comes our way. With Kid Cardula, I know I don't have to nurse him along. Also we decide on the strategy of letting the Kid get himself knocked down two, maybe three, times per fight. With this maneuver, we establish that while the Kid can hit, he ain't so good at taking a punch. Consequently every manager who's got a pug with a punch figures that his boy has got a good chance of putting the Kid away.

We get seven bouts in the next year, all of which the Kid wins by knockouts, of course, and we're drawing attention from other parts of the country.

Now that some money is beginning to come in, I expect the Kid to brighten up a little, which he does for about six months, but then I notice that he's starting to brood about something. I try to get him to tell me about it, but he just shakes his head.

Also, now that he's getting publicity, he begins to attract the broads. They really go for his type. He's polite to them and all that, and even asks them their addresses, but as far as I know he never follows up or pays them a visit.

One morning after we'd just won our tenth fight—a nine-round knockout over Irv Watson, who was on the way down, but still a draw —and I am sitting in my office dreaming about the day soon when I sell the gym or at least hire somebody to manage it, when there's a knock at the door.

The dame which enters and stands there looking scared is about your average height and weight, with average looks, and wearing good clothes. She's got black hair and a nose that's more than it should be. In all, nothing to get excited about.

She swallows hard. "Is this where I can find Mr. Kid Cardula?"

"He drops in every now and then," I say. "But it's not a schedule, never know when he'll turn up."

"Would you have his address?"

"No. He likes to keep that secret."

She looks lost for a few seconds and then decides to tell me what brought her here. "About two weeks ago I drove out of state to see my Aunt Harriet and when I came back, I got a late start and it got dark before I could make it home. I'm really not at all good with directions and it had been raining. I turned and turned, hoping that I'd find a road that looked familiar. Somehow I got on this muddy road and my car skidded right into a ditch. And I just couldn't get the car out. Finally I gave up and sat there, waiting for some car to pass, but there was no traffic at all. I couldn't even see a farmhouse light. I guess I finally fell asleep. I had the strangest dream, but I can't remember now exactly what it was, and when I woke, there was this tall distinguished-looking man standing beside the open door of my car and staring down at me. He gave me quite a start at first, but I recovered and asked him if he'd give me a lift to someplace where I could get to a phone and call my father and have him send someone out to pick me up. His car was parked on the road and he drove me to a crossroads where there was a gas station open."

I notice that she's got what look like two big mosquito bites on one side of her throat.

She goes on. "Anyway, while I was making the phone call, he drove away before I could thank him or get his name. But I kept thinking about . . ." She blushed. "Then last night while I was watching the late news, there were things about sports and a picture of Kid Cardula appeared on the TV screen, and immediately I knew that this must be the stranger who had driven me to the gas station. So I asked around and somebody told me that you were his manager and gave me the address of your gym. And I just thought I'd drop in and thank him in person."

I nod. "I'll pass the thanks on to the Kid the next time I see him."

She still stands there, thinking, and suddenly brightens again. "Also I wanted to return something to him. A money clip. With one thousand dollars in it. It was found beside my car when the tow truck went up to pull it out of the ditch."

Sure, I think. Some nice honest tow truck driver finds a thousand bucks on the ground and he doesn't put it in his own pocket But I nod again. "So give me the thousand and I'll see that the Kid gets it."

She laughs a little. "Unfortunately I forgot to bring the money and the clip with me." She opens her purse and yakes out a ball-point pen and some paper. "My name is Carrington. Daphne Carrington. I'll write the directions on how to get to our place. It's a bit complicated We call it Carrington Eyrie. Perhaps you've heard of it? It was featured in *Stately Home and Formal Garden Magazine* last year. Mr. Cardula will have to come in person, of course. So that he can identify the clip. "

When Kid Cardula drops in the next evening, I tell him about Daphne Carrington and give him the slip of paper she left.

The Kid frowns. "I didn't lose a thousand dollars. Besides, I never use a money clip."

I grin. "I thought not. But still she's willing to ante up a thousand bucks to meet you. Is any part of her story true?"

"Well ... I did drive her to that filling station after I. . . after I found her asleep in the car."

"I didn't know you owned a car."

"I bought it last week. There are some places just too far to fly."

"What model is it?"

"A 1974 Volkswagen. The motor's in good condition, but the body needs a little work." He sits on the corner of my desk, his eyes thoughtful. "She was driving a Lincoln Continental."

"Don't worry about it, Kid. Pretty soon you'll be driving Lincoln Continentals, too."

We begin spacing out our fights now. No bum-of-the-month stuff. Mostly because we're getting better quality opponents and also because it needs time and publicity to build up the interest and the big gates.

We win a couple more fights, which get television coverage, and the Kid should be happy, but he's still brooding.

And then one night he shows up in my office and he makes an announcement. "Manny, I'm getting married."

I'm a little astounded, but I see no threat. Lots of fighters are married. "Who's the lucky lady?"

"Daphne Carrington."

I think awhile before the name connects. "You mean *that* Daphne Carrington?"

He nods.

I stare at him. "I hope you don't take this wrong, Kid, but the dame ain't exactly Raquel Welch, even in the face department."

His chin gets stubborn. "She has a tremendous personality."

That I doubt too. "Kid," I say, "be honest with yourself. She ain't your type."

"She soon will be."

Suddenly the nub of the situation seems to flash into my mind and I'm shocked. "Kid, you're not marrying this dame for her money, are you?"

He looks away. "Manny, I have been getting letters from my relatives and many concerned friends. But especially relatives. It seems that they have heard or been told about my ring appearances. And they all point out—rather strongly—that for a man with my background, it is unthinkable that I should be appearing in a prize ring."

He still didn't look at me. "I have been thinking this over for a long time, Manny, and I am afraid they are right. I shouldn't be a boxer. Certainly not a professional. All of my family and all of my friends strongly disapprove. And, Manny, one must have one's own self-respect and the approval of one's peers if one wants to achieve any happiness in this world."

"Peers?" I say. "You mean like royalty? You a count or something? You got blue blood in your veins?"

"Occasionally." He sighs. "My relatives have even begun a collection to save me from destitution. But I cannot accept charity from relatives."

"But you don't mind marrying a dame for her money?"

"My dear Manny," he says. "Marrying a woman for her money is as good a reason as any. Besides, it will enable me to quit the fight game."

We argue and argue and I beg him to think it over for a while, telling him what all that ring money could mean to him—and me.

Finally he seems to give in a little, and when he leaves, he at least promises to think it over for a while.

About a week passes. I don't hear from him and I'm a nervous wreck. Finally, at around ten-thirty one evening, Alfie Bogan comes into my office with an envelope.

Right away I get the feeling that the envelope should have a black border. My fingers tremble when I open it and read the note from Kid Cardula.

> Dear Manny:
>
> I sincerely regret the way things have turned out, but I am determined to quit the ring. I know tht you pinned a great deal of hope on my future and I am certain that, under different circumstances, we would have made those millions you talked about.
>
> But goodbye and good luck. I have, however, decided not to leave you empty-handed.
>
> Best wishes,
> Kid Cardula.

Not leave me empty-handed? Did he enclose a nice little check? I shake the envelope, but nothing comes out. What the hell did he mean he wouldn't leave me empty-handed?

I glare at Alfie Bogan, who's still standing there.

He grins. "Hit me."

I stare. Somehow Alfie looks different. He has these two big mosquito bites on his throat and these two long upper teeth, which I swear I never seen before.

"Hit me," he says again.

Maybe I shouldn't do it, but it's been a long hard week of disappointments. So I let him have it with all I got.

And break my hand.

But I'm smiling when the doc puts on the cast.

I got me a replacement for Kid Cardula.

The Cardula
Detective Agency

I yawned, rubbed the stubble of my beard, and reflected once again what a boring and basically awkward process it was for me to shave myself every evening. Janos—my man—had done the task for me until two months ago, when I had had to let him go. I simply could not afford to feed him any longer.

I climbed out of bed and went to the dark windows. It was raining heavily. Certainly no weather for flying.

I plugged in my electric razor and went to work. I was becoming a bit more skilled at the job. Actually, of course, putting a straight part in my hair was much more difficult. When I finished shaving, I slipped out of my pajamas and showered.

I moved on to the closet and surveyed my two remaining suits, top quality, certainly, but both had seen better days. I sincerely hoped that some night soon I might replenish my wardrobe with something new, possibly even other than black.

I finished dressing and donned my black raincoat. I checked to make certain that I carried my tobacco pouch. There was no telling where circumstances might force me to spend the day.

Outside my apartment building, I raised my umbrella and began walking toward my office, slightly more than a mile away.

The rain slackened to a light drizzle as I proceeded down Wisconsin Avenue, crossed the bridge, and turned into the alley shortcut I usually take when I find it necessary to walk.

I had almost reached the opposite street—East Wells—when someone leaped upon me from behind, hooking his arm under my chin.

Clearly I was being mugged.

I reached back, grasped his collar, and flipped him head over heels some twenty feet into the side of a brick wall, from which point he dropped to the alley surface and remained still.

But apparently he was not alone. Another and larger figure sprang from a building recess and threw an overhand right which caught me squarely on the jaw. I distinctly heard several phalanges of his fist fracture and he yelped with surprise at the injury.

I then lifted him high overhead and sent him crashing across the alley to join his inert companion.

I brushed off my raincoat, picked up my umbrella, and continued on to my office. *Really*, I thought, *this was outrageous*. It was no longer safe for an innocent pedestrian to walk the streets or alleys at night.

When I reached my office, I found a young woman, probably in her late twenties, waiting at my office door.

She seemed a bit startled when she first saw me, but then most people are. She looked at the keys in my hand. "Do you work for the Cardula Detective Agency?"

I smiled sparingly. "I am the Cardula Detective Agency." I unlocked the door and we entered my one-room office.

She sat down, produced a silver case, and offered me a cigarette.

"No, thank you," I said. "I don't smoke."

She lit her cigarette. "My name is Olivia Hampton. I phoned about an hour ago. A recording said that your office hours are from eight P.M. to six A.M.?"

I nodded. "They vary according to the solstices."

"It's my Uncle Hector," she said. "Someone shot at him while he was dressing for dinner. The bullet went through his bedroom window and missed him by inches."

"Hmm," I said thoughtfully. "Since you came to me, I gather that you decided not go to the police."

"We regard the incident as a family matter. All of the logical suspects are relatives. Except for Uncle Custis Clay Finnegan. I mean, he's a relative, but not one of the suspects, because he has millions of his own."

"Why does anyone want your Uncle Hector dead?"

"Because he's going to change his will tomorrow morning when he sees his lawyer. He called us into the study and told us that he was cutting all of us out of his will."

"Why would he want to do that?"

"He said he just read a book and now he doesn't believe in individuals inheriting wealth. He's going to give his money to various parties."

"How much money does he have?

"The last time he mentioned the subject, I think he said three million."

"Aha, and you want me to find out who's trying to kill him?"

"If you can, of course. But the main idea is for you to see that Uncle Hector is still alive when he sees his lawyer at nine tomorrow morning. After that, there won't be any motive for any of us to kill him because we'll be out of the will anyway."

I drummed my fingers for a moment or two. "I'm afraid I can guarantee his safety only until approximately six A.M. tomorrow. After that I have another commitment."

She thought about that. "Well, it's better than nothing, I suppose. I don't imagine I could get anybody else at this time of the night." She got up. "I think we'd better get going right away. If anyone's going to murder Uncle Hector, it's got to happen tonight. I have a car and chauffeur waiting downstairs."

It was still drizzling when we walked half a block and turned into the parking lot.

As we approached a Volkswagen minibus, the driver's door burst open and a small uniformed chauffeur hopped out. He rushed forward and kissed the back of my hand.

It was Janos.

"Count," he breathed fervently. "It is so wonderful to see ya again."

Olivia smiled. "It was Janos who recommended that I come to you. Did he call you Count?"

I shrugged. "That was yesterday and today is today."

"His Highness has fallen on bad times," Janos said, "through no fault of his own."

I sighed. "At one time the subject of money never disturbed my mind. I had extensive holdings in Cuba, the Belgian Congo, Lebanon, Angola, and Bangladesh. What wasn't confiscated or nationalized was destroyed."

Janos slid back the side door of the minibus. "In the old country the people's government has made his castle a state shrine. Busloads of school children and tourists stop there every day, and the grounds are sprinkled with souvenir and food stands. The entire lower east gallery has been converted to public restrooms."

As Olivia and I rode in the back of the minibus, she gave me some background on the members of Uncle Hector's household. There were Cousin Albert, whose right arm was three inches longer than his left and Cousin Maggie, who liked red port, and Cousin Wendy, who wrote the kindest rejection slips, and Cousin Fairbault, who detested crustaceans.

After some twenty miles of freeway travel, we took an off-ramp and continued on a two-lane road into the countryside, where only an occasional farmyard light broke the darkness.

It began to rain heavily again. Lightning flashed across the sky and thunder rolled—truly a splendid evening.

It was nearly ten-thirty when we turned in at a pair of gateposts and followed the graveled and bumpy driveway through a cordon of grotesque, bare-branched trees. In the revelation of another bolt of lightning I saw ahead the looming monster of a Victorian mansion. Here and there a light gleamed dully from behind pulled drapes.

Janos stopped the Volkswagen and Olivia and I rushed up the wide steps to the shelter of the porch. She opened a huge door and we stepped into the large, dimly lit vestibule.

I heard a muffled crash from somewhere deep inside the house followed almost instantly by a brief series of splinterings. *Strange*, I thought, *it sounded exactly like a bowling alley.*

"I'll introduce you all around," Olivia said. "And we might just as well start with Albert." She led me through a passageway and then down a flight of stairs to high-ceilinged cellars.

I looked about as we proceeded. Stone walls, stone floors, roomy, damp, musty-smelling, grimed by a century of dampened dust.

I heard the crashing noise again, this time much closer.

Olivia opened a door and we stepped into the bright lights of an elongated room containing a two-lane bowling alley.

A gangly man in his thirties, concentrating intensely, stood poised to bowl. He took a five-step approach and delivered the ball smoothly with a flawless follow-through. The ball hit the pins solidly, and he had a strike.

The automatic pin-spotter scooped up the pins and returned the ball.

"Albert," Olivia said, "this is Mr. Cardula. He's a private detective and he's spending the night with us to see that Uncle Hector doesn't get killed."

Albert shook hands, but he seemed eager to get back to his bowling.

I glanced at his score sheet. He had a string of seven strikes. I nodded approvingly. "What is your average?"

He brightened. "I have 257 over the last one thousand games."

Was he pulling my leg? A 257 average? I smiled slightly. "Magnificent bowling."

He agreed. "I practice ten hours a day. I would make it more, but that's about all the bowling the human body can take."

I glanced down. Yes, his right arm did seem to be several inches longer than his left.

"When I'm not bowling," Albert said, "I do all of the maintenance work down here. I can even take the pin-spotters apart and put them back together blindfolded." He smiled. "I have 983 perfect games so far."

Nine hundred eitghty-three perfect games? Oh, come now, I thought.

But he nodded earnestly. "And the alleys aren't grooved or anything like that. They could pass inspection anytime by the American Bowling Congress."

When we left him, Olivia said, "Albert's father was something of a local bowling celebrity in his hometown. He and Albert's mother were killed in an automobile accident when Albert was ten. He spent six years in an orphanage before Uncle Hector heard about him and got him out. But by then ..." She sighed. "Uncle Hector had the alley built because bowling seemed to be the only thing that interested Albert."

I followed her through an archway. "Albert shouldn't have to brood about being cut out of the will. If what he says about his bowling is true, he is the greatest bowler this world has ever seen or is likely to see. He would sweep any tournament he entered, and what with endorsements and such, he could easily become a millionaire in a relative short time."

Olivia shook her head. "No. Albert has never left these grounds since the day he came here. He doesn't want to see any other part of the world, no matter what it has to offer."

She led me to another door and switched on a light.

I found myself gazing upon bushel baskets and boxes of apples, potatoes, beets, rutabagas, squashes, and bins of sand which I surmised contained carrots and other root vegetables. One side of the room was totally shelved and occupied by an array of glass jars containing preserved tomatoes, green and wax beans, and dozens of other fruits and vegetables. Two large top-loading freezers stood at one end of the room.

"Cousin Fairbault does all of this himself," Olivia said. "The seeding, the cultivating, the harvesting. Then he cans and freezes and preserves. He's converted the carriage house into a barn and he raises our beef, and pork, and chickens. He also makes sausages and ham and even cheeses."

She closed the door. "Fairbault was a Navy pilot. He got shot down and was washed ashore onto a tiny uninhabited island not more than one acre in size. It had three palm trees and all kinds of miscellaneous vegetation, but none of it edible. He couldn't even fish, because he had nothing to fish with. But there were spider crabs and slugs and all kinds of things that crawled and scuttled and came out mostly at night. Fairbault was on that island for seven years before he was rescued—he was down to eighty pounds. He spent another five years in an asylum where he tried to hoard food under his mattress."

We took the stairs up. "When Fairbault first came here, he kept that room locked at all times. We had to ask his permission whenever we wanted anything for the kitchen and he would watch over us while we got it. But he's been here eleven years now and he trusts us so much that he leaves the room unlocked and we are free to take anything we want at any time, just as long as we don't waste it."

We returned to the first floor and entered a large, well-ordered kitchen. In one corner, a heavyset woman in her fifties sat at a table working at a jigsaw puzzle. A half-empty bottle of red wine and a glass were at her elbow.

Olivia introduced me to Cousin Maggie. "She does the cooking for us and she's really the best cook in the world."

Maggie beamed. "I try to do the best I can and I don't touch a drop until seven. Are you hungry, Mr. Cardula? Could I fix you a snack?"

"No, thank you," I said. "I had something last week."

She blinked. "Last week?"

I cleared my throat. "I mean, I have taken nourishment lately enough not to be hungry. How do you feel about your Uncle Hector changing his will and leaving all of you out?"

Maggie shrugged. "Well, it's his money and I wasn't really counting on any part of it, even assuming that I would outlive him." Her eyes clouded with worry. "Just as long as I have my job here. That's all that really counts."

We left Maggie to her jigsaw puzzle and bottle and proceeded to the second floor.

"You employ a cousin to do the cooking?" I asked.

"Maggie likes to be useful."

"Why is she worried about the possibility of losing her job here? If she's as good a cook as you claim, she shouldn't have any difficulty getting another job. "

"Unfortunately, whenever she worked anywhere else, she began drinking as soon as she woke in the morning and kept it up as long as she was able to stand, or sit. She was continually getting fired without references and was in quite desperate straits when Uncle Hector found her."

Olivia stopped at an open doorway.

I looked into an abundantly furnished room. A plump, balding man sat comfortably ensconced in a deep easy chair, puffing a large curved pipe and engrossed in a book whose jacket read *Secrets with Broccoli.*

Olivia introduced me to Fairbault.

He offered me wine, but I declined.

He held his own glass to the light. "Six years in the cask. I call it Fairbault '71. Because of the climate here, I am forced to concentrate on the northern grapes. Not nearly as ideal for wine as the sweet California varieties, but one must make do."

I glanced at the bookshelves. All of the volumes seemed concerned with vegetable and fruit gardening and animal husbandry. One entire shelf contained what was very likely eleven years of an organic gardening magazine. "Do you do any green-housing?" I asked.

He shook his head. "No. Green-housing would expand the season to twelve months a year and too much is too much. Besides, half of the fun of gardening is to store and stock and preserve during the winter months and read gardening magazines and make plans for the spring."

We left Fairbault and continued down the corridor. We turned a corner and found a somewhat hefty and firm-jawed lady in her forties, nearly supine in a window seat, her face deathly white with perhaps a few touches of green. A cigar, one inch smoked, dangled from her somewhat limp square hand.

Olivia sighed. "Why don't you give up trying to smoke cigars, Wendy? You know you just can't do it."

Cousin Wendy opened her eyes. "One of these damn days I'll find the right brand."

"Cousin Wendy is the founder and editor of the *Trempleau County Poetry Review*. It has one hundred and ten subscribers from all over the country and one hundred and nine of them are also contributors."

Cousin Wendy nodded. "Believe me, it makes for a twelve-hour day. Last month I had to plow through eight hundred manuscripts before I could make up the November issue. But I suppose nobody really appreciates al the work I put in and the correspondence and the free constructive criticism."

"Now, Wendy," Olivia said, "you know that every one of your readers is absolutely depending on you to sift and winnow, to separate the wheat from the chaff." She turned to me. "Cousin Wendy is not only an editor, but she is also a top poetry person."

Cousin Wendy shrugged modestly. "I try to keep my hand in when I have the time."

When we left her, I said, "Trempleau County? Isn't that about three hundred miles north?"

"Yes. That's where Cousin Wendy used to live. She was a waitress in a roadside café and wrote poetry on the side. Then one day a trucker came on a batch of her poems and started reading them out loud to the customers. So she crushed his skull with a counter stool. She was still in prison when Uncle Hector heard about her and he vouched for her at the parole hearing."

"Just one moment, I said. "Are you telling me that all of these people are really blood relatives of Uncle Hector?"

Olivia sighed and smiled faintly. "Well, to tell the truth, none of us really is. But we like to think of ourselves as cousins because it's warmer."

We went downstairs this time.

"Uncle Custis is our houseguest about once every six months or so," Olivia said. "He came here after supper tonight and Uncle Hector insisted that none of us breathe a word about the murder attempt on his life. He doesn't want Uncle Custis to worry. So I'll just tell Uncle Custis that you are also a houseguest."

We found Uncles Hector and Custis at a pool table in the game room.

Uncle Hector, a short man with soft white hair, had good nature stamped into his face.

Uncle Custis, on the other hand, was tall and gimlet-eyed. He regarded me sourly. 'A houseguest? Or are you another one of those damn cousins Hector digs up now and then?"

"How much has Uncle Custis won from you so far this evening?" Olivia asked.

Uncle Hector shrugged. "Fifteen dollars."

"Uncle Custis is quite a pool player," Olivia said. "Eight ball is his favorite game."

"Eight ball?" I said. "Is that anything like billiards? I remember in my student years at the university I played the game a number of times."

Uncle Custis eyed me pityingly for a moment. Then he allowed himself an economical smile and explained to me the simple rules of eight ball. "Would you care to try your hand at it? I like to make things little more interesting. How does five dollars a game strike you?"

I lost the first game, and the second.

Uncle Custis consulted his watch. "I'm just about ready for bed. What do you say about a final game? Let's make it for fifty dollars?"

I agreed and then proceeded to win that game with the utmost skill and dispatch.

Uncle Custis watched as I bank-shot the eight ball into the side pocket and then glared. "I've been hustled. I know when I've been hustled." He flung five tens onto the table and stormed out of the room.

Uncle Hector regarded me with approval. "Damn, I've been wanting to do that for years."

I turned to business. "Sir, if you don't mind my saying so, wouldn't it have been wiser to change your will secretly and then inform your household that it had been disinherited? Do you realize how many people who boldly and blatantly announce that they are going to change their wills the first thing in the morning never get to see the sun rise?" I winced slightly at the last two words.

"Nonsense," Uncle Hector said. "Ninety-nine percent of will changers survive to see their lawyers the next morning. The one percent, who are murdered, get all of the publicity and give the entire process a bad name." He glanced at the wall clock. "Well, I suppose it's bedtime for all of us too. I understand that you are going to keep watch outside of my bedroom door tonight?"

"No," I said firmly. "I will be inside your bedroom. I do not intend to allow you out of my sight for one moment."

We said good-night to Olivia and went upstairs.

Hector's bedroom was quite as large as my entire apartment and contained a huge canopy bed and a capacious fireplace.

While Hector changed to pajamas, I searched the room thoroughly. then went to the windows and checked to make certain that they were all securely locked. I drew the drapes and sat down.

I frowned. There was something wrong here. Something I should have seen, but didn't. My eyes went over the room again, but I simply couldn't put my finger on it.

Hector sat on the bed and took off his slippers. "There's really no need for you to stay up all night. Why not lie down on that couch? I could get you a pillow and some blankets."

"No, thank you," I said. I went to the bookshelves, found a volume on hematology, and sat down.

Hector climbed into bed and closed his eyes. After five minutes he turned restlessly. He repeated the turnings at fairly regular intervals. Finally he sighed and sat up. "I simply can't go to sleep without my regular glass of warm milk and tonight I completely forgot about it. You wouldn't care to slip down to the kitchen and see if Maggie is still up? If she isn't, could you put a glass of milk into a saucepan and heat it slowly? Short of boiling, you know. And then add a teaspoon of sugar and a few dashes of cinnamon?"

"I'm sorry," I said. "But I am not leaving this room."

He thought it over. "Then I think I'll just hop down there myself."

"Very well," I said, "but I will accompany you. And we will make certain that the milk is taken from a fresh sealed bottle."

Hector scratched the back of his neck. "Forget it. It's too far to the kitchen anyway." He brightened. "There's a liquor cabinet over there. Why don't you help yourself to something? There's nothing like a good snort or two for relaxation."

"I do not intend to relax," I said. "And besides, I do not drink. At least not liquor."

Hector sank back onto his pillow and closed his eyes.

The hours passed. It was somewhat after five in the morning when I suddenly realized what it was that I should have seen earlier, but didn't.

I looked in Hector's direction. Was he really asleep or was he faking it?

I allowed five minutes to pass, then yawned and let my eyelids droop and finally close, except for a calculated millimeter or two. I began breathing heavily and allowed the book to slip from my hands to the carpeted floor.

Uncle Hector's eyes opened and he watched me intently for perhaps three minutes. Then he slipped quietly out of bed and tiptoed over to a bureau. He opened a drawer and removed a Finnish-style hunting knife.

I tensed a bit, but he crept past me to the door and disappeared into the hall.

I rose and followed him.

As he threaded through the halls, he looked back frequently, but I kept myself confined to the darkness of the high ceiling.

He paused before a door, slowly turned its knob, and crept inside. I silently swooped into the room myself.

The room was very much like the one he had left. It too was graced by a canopy bed and upon it lay Uncle Custis, gently snoring.

Hector approached the bed and raised the dagger high into the air.

I quickly sprang forward, grasped his wrist, and removed the knife from his grip. He was startled at my appearance and action, but he made no exclamation. He merely closed his eyes for a moment.

On the bed, Uncle Custis continued his snoring without interruption.

I moved to one of the windows and pushed aside the drape for a moment. It was still raining heavily and the lightning periodically fractured the dark sky. Exhilarating.

I let the drapes fall back into position, motioned to Hector, and we went back into the hall.

On our way back to his room, Uncle Hector glanced at the ceiling now and then. "You know, I could have sworn I caught just a glimpse of something flying up there a little while ago."

Once inside his room, I said, "Aha, the old bedroom-switch ploy."

He portrayed innocence. "What old bedroom-switch ploy?"

"When I first came into this room and searched it, I should have seen something, but it was not there. If it had been there, I would certainly have noticed it immediately. It took me a bit of time to realize it was not there, but once I did, I suspected that there was mischief afoot and that you were probably at the root of it."

"What are you talking about?"

"Olivia came to me because someone took a shot at you through your bedroom window." I pointed in the direction of the windows, "Neither one of those has a bullet hole in it."

He thought fiercely and then smiled. "I forgot to mention that the window was open at the time."

"Good try," I acknowledged. "But then how do you explain the fact that one of the windows in the room Custis now occupies does have a bullet hole in it?"

He resumed thinking, but I cut the effort short. "You faked that attempt on your life and this evening you probably told Custis that his regular guest room was being painted, or something of the sort, and he should take your bedroom instead."

"Why would I do that?"

"Because you intended to murder Custis and make it appear as though the crime had occurred by accident. Someone in the house, thinking that you still occupied your own bed, sneaked into the room, and in the darkness mistook Uncle Custis for you, and stabbed him to death."

Hector evaded my eyes and said nothing.

"Why?" I asked. "Why were you trying to murder Custis?"

He finally sighed. "Money, of course."

"But you've got millions."

"I had millions. Good solid investments in Angola, Lebanon, Bangladesh ..." He shrugged. "Today I am almost dead broke."

Now his eyes met mine. "You have seen and talked to the people who inhabit this house?"

I nodded.

"Then you know that they have all been severely wounded by the world we live in. If they had to return to it, they would break completely. And I really couldn't allow that to happen. So I decided that the only way I could get enough money to keep this household going was to kill Custis. Basically he's a mean bastard anyway and wouldn't be missed by anyone. And we really are cousins, you know. Custis has no visible heirs other than me, so if he should die, I would certainly get first crack at his estate. You don't suppose you could let me have the knife again so I could finish ..."

"No," I said firmly.

And yet I could sympathize with Uncle Hector. He had a duty and a responsibility to the members of the household.

Hector needed and deserved help. I sighed. All right. I would do the job for him. Not tonight or in this house, of course. But some evening a week or two from now when Custis walked a city street I would leap upon him, snap his neck, and remove his wallet. The crime would he put down in the police records as a fatal mugging.

I put my hand on Hector's shoulder. "I absolutely insist that you put the idea of murdering Custis completely out of your mind. I have the strongest premonition that your fortune will change dramatically within a week or two."

Hector seemed ready to wait. "To tell you the truth, I'm a little relieved that I didn't go through with it tonight."

I glanced at my wristwatch. It was that time again.

I went to the window and pulled aside the drapes. Still raining. A bad night for fliers. I turned to Hector. "You don't suppose that Janos could drive me back to the city?"

"Of course. His room is on the third floor, right next to the bust of Edgar Allan Poe."

I went up to the third floor and woke Janos with my request.

He yawned and consulted his alarm clock. "I'm sorry, Your Highness, but in wet weather like this, water condenses in the distributor of our Volkswagen. By the time I got everything apart and wiped dry and put together and the engine perhaps started, we would never be able tot make it to the city in time. And the minibus is the only vehicle we have."

Damn, I thought, that leaves me no alternative but getting wet. If I leave right now I might have time for a hot footbath when I get to my apartment.

"Why don't you stay here?" Janos said. "There's a nice roomy place in the cellar. I could fix up an army cot. I am certain that nobody would disturb you down there."

We carried what we needed downstairs to a large chamber in the cellar. Janos unfolded the cot and put a mattress on top of it. "Your tobacco pouch, sir?"

I handed it to him. "It isn't necessary to sprinkle the stuff all over the mattress anymore, Janos. I discovered that simply putting the full pouch under the pillow will suffice. I suppose it is the spirit of the thing rather than the letter that counts."

Janos finished putting on the sheets, the pillowcases, and the blankets. "Have a nice sleep, sir."

When he was gone, I slipped into the pajamas and lay down. Really a most spacious chamber. Beautiful vaulting at the doorway. The aroma of damp, stagnant air. I could almost imagine what the place would look like if I brought in a few choice items of furnishings from my apartment.

I sighed. But it was not to be. This was a strange household, but was really expecting too much of its occupants to accept me.

I thought I heard a noise in the passageway outside.

I put on my slippers and hid in the shadows near the archway.

Olivia passed by outside. She wore a dressing gown, slippers, and from the turban-like creation on her head, I guessed that she had her hair in curlers.

She opened a door at the end of the passageway.

I saw a room elegant with draped antique spiderwebs and in the center of it, on a marble pedestal, stood a magnificent, comfortable-looking sarcoph—

Olivia entered the room and closed the door behind her. After a few tense moments, I distinctly heard the creak of a lid rising. And then lowering.

I smiled and went back to my cot.

I don't care what tradition demands, I always sleep on my left side.

The Canvas Caper

"Mr. Cardula," he said, "how do you feel about blackmailers?"

"They are dastardly people, sir."

He gazed out of the window at the scattered lights in the office building across the street. "Frankly, they should be dead, don't you think?"

"Possibly, sir."

He turned his back to me. "I drew the low card."

My prospective client was a tall man dressed with impeccable elegance. There was also the faint aura of liquor about him.

He continued. "We cut cards and I got the three of clubs which left the job up to me. It was all to be simple and direct. I would enter his home and shoot him. And if, for some fantastic reason, they should question me, the others would swear that I had never left the table all evening."

"The table?"

"The card table. They would claim that I had never left the room all evening."

"They?"

"My associates in this matter." He sighed. "I went so far as to knock at his door, but then I turned and ran before he opened it."

He looked out of the window again. "What would you say if I offered you ten thousand dollars to kill someone? Or to find someone who would? I suppose you'd go to the police?"

I smiled faintly. "If I did, I could prove nothing. It would be my word against yours that the offer was ever made."

He remained thoughtful for a few moments. "Frankly, I don't know any killers for hire or how to go about finding them. But then it came to me that private detectives generally muck about in the seamier things of life, what with divorce work, wiretapping, and so forth, and if anyone knew of an available killer, they certainly should. Anyway, it appeared to be my only lead to the underworld. So I turned to the yellow pages of the phonebook for help."

"And why did you select me?"

"It seemed to me that any private detective whose office hours are from eight P.M. to four A.M. must be closer to the night world of crime than anybody else."

I contemplated my bridged fingertips. "Perhaps I can help you at that. What would be the exact financial arrangement for this killing?"

He brightened and leaned forward. "I don't have that much money on me right now, but I will see that you get five thousand tomorrow and the other five thousand when the job is done."

I nodded. "And what is your name, sir?"

"Never mind that. It won't be necessary for you to know."

"Well then, the name of the victim. I certainly wouldn't want to kill the wrong man, sir."

"His name is Raoul Henri O'Brien, at 118 Frawley Road." My client sighed. "An artist. Of sorts."

"He is blackmailing you and your associates?"

"Yes."

"About what?"

"I don't think it is necessary to your job to know why."

I accepted that. "Undoubtedly you will want to arrange an alibi for the time O'Brien dies. When do you want him killed?"

He thought about it. "How about Friday evening? Anywhere from, say, eight to eleven?"

"It is as good as done, sir. Provided, of course, that I receive the first five thousand dollars tomorrow."

He nodded and rose. "As a private detective, I suppose that you are rather good at following people?"

"Sir, that is my speciality. I am superb at it."

"Fine. But don't try to follow me. You will stand at that window and look out. When I reach the street, I will look back up. If I do not see you still at the window, I will assume that you are attempting to follow me and the whole deal will be off. I will find somebody else to earn the ten thousand dollars."

When he left, I went to the window as directed and looked down at the lighted street four stories below. At this time of night—nearly eleven—the street was almost deserted.

I saw my client leave the building and cross the street. He stopped and looked back up.

I waved.

He acknowledged this with a nod and continued walking. He turned the corner and disappeared.

I opened my window and followed.

I had, of course, not the slightest intention of murdering Raoul O'Brien. However, as I had pointed out to my client, taking the matter to the police would be futile. I had to know more about the conspiracy and its participants before I could act in an effective manner.

I sighted my client again as he slipped into an automobile parked at the curb.

He drove from the central city to Lake Shore Road and on to the sub-urbs. Eventually he turned into a long, graveled driveway. I paused at the roadside mailbox long enough to read the name JAMES MCQUIGG-LEY and then continued after.

My client parked his car behind three other vehicles before a large Norman-style home. He opened the front door and entered.

I moved on to the side of the building where light streamed from a slightly opened French window. Inside I saw three men seated at a card table.

One of them looked a bit familiar. Ah, yes. The short, round man in his middle fifties would be Florian Appleby of the Appleby Galler-ies. I had sold him the last two paintings I had managed to bring over to America.

I sighed. When I fled the old country, I had managed to take but a few things with me—some gold, a few pieces of jewelry, and a half dozen paintings—whatever could be fitted, somewhat uncomfortably, in an eight-by-three-foot box.

But, alas, all of my possessions were now gone and I was forced to work for a livelihood.

All three of the men at the card table looked up eagerly as my cli-ent entered the room.

"Well, James," Appleby said, "is Raoul dead?"

My client—apparently James McQuiggley—went to the liquor cab-inet and poured himself a drink. "Raoul is still alive. I couldn't bring myself to kill him."

Appleby registered his disappointment. "You reneged, James. I can't stand a man who reneges."

McQuiggley shrugged. "I have come up with a much more satis-factory solution to our problem. I managed to hire a professional killer who will do the job for us."

Appleby regarded him with some awe. "How in the world did you know where to contact a professional killer?"

McQuiggley smiled mysteriously. "I have my ways. He is asking ten thousand dollars to do the job. We must each ante up one-fourth."

He sipped his drink. "He is going to kill Raoul sometime between eight and eleven this coming Friday evening, so we will all gather here again during those hours."

When Appleby and the two others left, I journeyed to 118 Frawley Road, approximately a half mile farther on.

The address proved to be a huge Victorian structure in the midst of wooded acreage. I glided silently to the only lighted windows. A strikingly handsome woman, perhaps in her early thirties, sat watching the late movie on a television screen.

I heard a car coming up the driveway and moved back to the front of the house.

A Karmann Ghia pulled to a stop and a trimly bearded young man stepped out. He used a key to unlock the front door.

I hied back to the window in time to see him enter the room. The woman barely looked up for a moment and then resumed her television viewing. As for the man —Raoul Henri O'Brien?—he continued through the room and up a stairway.

Light appeared from two windows upstairs and I watched O'Brien change to pajamas, yawn, and lie down on a bed where he promptly fell asleep.

I returned to the woman downstairs and became engrossed in the motion picture she was watching—something about a creature from a dark lagoon.

At the conclusion of the movie, she turned off the set and went upstairs to another bedroom.

I left her to her privacy and flitted about the outside of the building, peering into dark windows here and there (my eyesight remains rather keen even under the darkest of circumstances.) At the rear of the house I found what had very likely once been a solarium was now converted into an artist's studio.

My exploration done, I returned to my office, closed the window, and consulted the yellow pages of my phonebook until I found that there existed a James McQuiggley Art Gallery.

So both McQuiggley and Appleby dealt in paintings and their intended victim was an artist. Of sorts, McQuiggley had qualified. Then it was a fair assumption that the other two gentlemen I'd seen in the McQuiggley's home were also connected with the world of art in one capacity or another?

Raoul Henri O'Brien. Was he an artist? Frankly, I'd never heard of him before.

The next evening at eight P.M. when I reached my office, I found a small package had been thrust through the mail slot in the door.

I opened it and found five thousand dollars in one-hundred-dollars bills.

Should I go to the police now? Or would it be wiser to learn more about the entire matter before I made such a move? Perhaps if I asked O'Brien a few judicious questions, I could learn why McQuiggley and his associates wanted him killed.

I returned to 118 Frawley Road and pressed the doorbell.

The woman who had watched the TV screen the previous evening answered the door. "Yes?"

"Could I speak to Mr. O'Brien, please?"

She had speculative gray eyes. "I'm sorry, but he's not here. He left about an hour ago."

"Could you tell me when he will return?"

"I haven't the faintest idea."

Would you by any chance know where he has gone?"

"He didn't tell me and I didn't ask."

She looked past my shoulder. "Where's your car?"

I cleared my throat. "I parked it down the road a bit."

There seemed to be nothing more to do but say goodbye and I did. I walked down the driveway and glanced back. She still watched me from the doorway, so I continued until I was well out of sight.

What should I do now? On the assumption that O'Brien might return early, should I linger about the premises and wait? I decided that it was worth a try and made my way stealthily back to the house and the lighted windows.

The room was empty of human life, but only for a few minutes. Then a woman entered carrying a sandwich on a small plate and a glass of milk. She turned on the TV set and sat down.

We settled down to watch what the screen had to offer, which, until ten o'clock consisted primarily of squealing tires and endless automobile chases.

After the ten o'clock news, she switched channels to the late movie, *Werewolf in the Tower of London*—really quite engrossing.

At its conclusion, she turned off the set and retired to her bedroom.

It was now nearly one o'clock in the morning. Should I continue my vigil? The dark sky threatened rain and I detest getting wet. I decided to make a run, so to speak, for my office and I arrived there just as the first heavy drops began to fall.

The next evening—a Thursday—I rose as usual just after sunset, I showered, dressed, and settled down to read the newspaper before setting off for my office.

An item on an inside page instantly caught my attention.

A Raoul Henri O'Brien, 118 Frawley Road, had been killed by a hit-and-run driver at eleven-thirty the previous night as he left a supper club. According to witnesses, O'Brien had been crossing the street when an automobile had come speeding out of the darkness and struck him. The impact tossed him more than sixty feet and he was killed instantly. The witnesses were unable to recall the automobile's license number, but the vehicle was described as being a light-colored late-model Lincoln Continental.

I frowned. Had McQuiggley or one of his associates decided to take the bit into his own teeth and dispose of O'Brien? Or was this a legitimate hit-and-run accident?

When I reached my office, I found another brown package on the floor inside. It too contained five thousand dollars in one-hundred-dollar-bills.

Clearly all of this needed further investigation. I went to McQuiggley's home and pressed the buzzer at the door.

McQuiggley himself answered. He showed alarm when he saw me. "Good heavens, there was no need for you to come here. I dropped off he second five thousand at your office this afternoon."

"I know. However, I have a few questions to ask."

The murmur of voices from within indicated that McQuiggley had guests. He quickly pulled me into a side room. "Our agreement was that O'Brien was to be killed on Friday, not Wednesday. It was just good luck that yesterday was Charlie's wedding anniversary and we were all at the party. Otherwise I doubt if any one of us would have an alibi."

Charlie? I remembered that when I'd gone to the yellow pages I had also seen a Charles Hanson Galleries listed. "Have the police questioned you?"

"No. I really don't expect them to. I just like to be prepared." He smiled. "Frankly I thought you'd use a gun or a knife or a blunt instrument, but I suppose hit-and-run was more intelligent." Another thought came to him. "How did you know where to find me?"

I flicked a professional smile. "McQuiggley, I know all about your group—you, Appleby, Hanson, and—the one with the beard. His name is at the tip of my tongue."

McQuiggley supplied it. "Brinkmann."

Ah yes. Hadn't I also seen a Brinkmann Galleries in the yellow pages? I seated myself. "Mr. McQuiggley, I did not kill your Raoul O'Brien."

He blinked. "You didn't? But if you didn't, who did?"

"I haven't the faintest idea. Why was O'Brien trying to blackmail you?"

"That is none of your business."

"I am tempted to go to the police and tell them what has transpired between us."

"I would deny everything."

"Really, sir? Then how would you explain to the police the fact that your fingerprints are on the ten thousand dollars I have in my safe?"

Actually, I had no knowledge as to whether McQuiggley had or had not left his fingerprints on the money.

He rubbed his chin reflectively. "Couldn't you just keep the money and forget about the whole thing?"

I shrugged. "Perhaps if I learn the truth, I might not find it necessary to go to the police."

McQuiggley sighed and then capitulated. "Very well. We first met O'Brien two years ago when he arrived here from the West Coast and here presented himself as a connoisseur and collector of modern paintings. He attended all the exhibitions and parties and even bought a painting here and there. He certainly had an engaging personality and he simply wormed himself into the art world here.

"Periodically he would dash off to Europe for two or three weeks and when he returned it was always with original paintings which he claimed he had purchased from private galleries or discovered in out-of-the-way pawnshops and attics. He would add them to his own collection and at various times showed them to each one of us.

"Naturally the estimated value of his paintings came into our conversations and he very cleverly left the impression that while he was quite sharp about the value of his Cézannes, he was more than a bit hazy concerning his van Goghs, Gauguins, Modiglianis, and so forth."

McQuiggley wiped his forehead with a handkerchief. "And so it appeared that here was a golden opportunity for us to pick up paintings at bargain prices and turn a penny or two."

"And what with one thing, and another, each of us bought canvases, which he reluctantly, very reluctantly, let go. For friendship's sake, so to speak. In all, over a period of two years, I bought fourteen paintings from him, and my associates perhaps a similar number each."

"And in turn you sold them to someone else?"

He brightened slightly. "At a modest profit, of course."

"But then something went wrong?"

"Yes, A week ago O'Brien told us that the paintings we had purchased were forgeries, every last one of them. And the reason he knew that they were forgeries was simply because he had painted them himself."

McQuiggley shook his head sadly. "I grudgingly admit that, as a forger, he was a genius. He took us all in completely. Fooled the eye and what modest tests we made. He had a good thing going, but unfortunately he was also greedy. He wanted more money than what the canvases brought him and he threatened to reveal the forgeries unless we agreed to pay him an additional one hundred thousand dollars each."

"Why didn't you go to the police?"

He seemed pained that I should ask such a question.

"The exposure would have absolutely ruined us. Our reputation for business. Not to mention people clamoring for their money back and threatening to sue."

"But still you decided that you were not going to pay O'Brien for his silence?"

McQuiggley nodded. "There was the possibility that he would come back to us again and again with demands for more money, and it also remained that O'Brien *alive* could blow the whistle on us at any time, if only in a careless moment."

I pondered. "All of you—Appleby. Hanson, Brinkmann,—and you have alibis for the time O'Brien was killed."

"We were on Charlie's yacht. We took a moonlight cruise that began at eight P.M. and lasted until well past three A.M. It would have been impossible for any of us to have gotten off the ship to kill O'Brien, if that's what you are thinking."

"Was O'Brien married?"

"He never said he was."

"Then who is the woman living in his house?"

"That would be Louise Peterson. She was his secretary, or something of the sort. Mostly something of the sort, I would imagine."

I left McQuiggley and went on to 118 Frawley Road, where I pressed the doorbell.

Louise Peterson answered the door.

"My name is Cardula," I said. "Private investigator." I handed her one of my cards.

She examined it. "What is there to investigate?"

"The death of Raoul O'Brien."

She regarded me calmly. "Are you working for an insurance company?"

I smiled noncommittally. "Was Raoul O'Brien's life heavily insured? And who is the beneficiary?"

"As far as I know he didn't carry any insurance. Besides, who would he leave the money to? He didn't have any what you might call friends— or relatives."

"Possibly you might be his beneficiary?"

She laughed shortly. "Ha!"

"Madam," I said, "I have reason to believe that Raoul O'Brien was murdered."

She allowed me to enter the house.

"You were Raoul O'Brien's secretary?"

"You might say that."

"Then possibly you were aware of O'Brien's activities?"

"What activities?"

I thought I might as well come out into the open. "Blackmail, madam. Blackmail."

She eyed me skeptically. "Blackmail? Who the hell would he blackmail and why?"

"Art dealers, madam. Your employer sold a number of paintings to art dealers in this city and every last one of them is a forgery."

She folded her arms. "Really?"

"But was he satisfied with that?" I asked rhetorically. "No, he was not. After he sold the forgeries, he again approached the dealers and threatened to expose the entire racket if they did not each give him an additional one hundred thousand dollars."

She blinked. "The bastard."

"Greed is the undoing of many an enterprise," I said . "Raoul O'Brien was not content with just painting the canvases and selling them, he had to stoop to blackmail."

She stared at the ceiling. "The canvases were forgeries and O'Brien painted them?"

"He confessed the deception to the dealers when he approached them for the blackmail." I allowed a drop of acid to creep into my voice. "But surely. Madam, working for the man and residing in his house as you do, you could not have failed to notice that there was a bit of hanky-panky?"

She seemed to be thinking. "You don't suppose that one of those art dealers got into his car and ran down the dirty dog?"

"No, Madam. Every one of them has an ironclad alibi for the time of O'Brien's death."

She shrugged. "Or possibly you think that I might have killed the creep?"

"Madam," I said. "You have referred to the deceased as a bastard, a dirty dog, and a creep. I sense that you might have a motive for killing him. However, I know that you did not."

"How could you know that?"

I knew, of course, because at the time of O'Brien s death she and I had been watching *Werewolf in the Tower of London*, she in comfort and

I chilled to the bone. But I said, "Suffice it to say that I have an instinct about such matters."

She regarded me with interest. "If one of the wheeler-dealers didn't kill him and I didn't, whom does that leave? Could it have been a plain old-fashioned hit-and-run accident?

"At the moment it appears so."

She smiled slightly. "So you're a private detective? How does it pay?"

I shrugged. "It's a living."

"You've got a certain style," she said. "Yes, I believe you, sir."

I would have blushed except that I did not want to s rain

Her eyes steadied into mine. "Cardula, how would you like to take O'Brien's place?

"Madam," I said, somewhat shocked at the directness, "what are you proposing? O'Brien is not yet in the ground and already you are casting eyes. Perhaps if we waited a decent month or two—"

She went on. "Raoul was just my front. My salesman. Nothing more. You need a man to do the talking when you're negotiating with dealers. I painted those canvases."

My mouth dropped. "You! You painted those forgeries?"

She nodded. "Though technically they are not forgeries. They are originals done in the style of anybody you'd care to name. I have a knack for that sort of thing. If I can find space on my studio floor for a canvas, I'll whip you up a Jackson Pollock that will blow your mind."

"You mean that you—a *woman*—?"

"Why not? Is there a law against it? What is so ridiculous about a woman being an unscrupulous forger? I did the painting and O'Brien did the selling. But the blackmailing was his own idea. I didn't know a thing about it and may he fry in hell."

She came closer. "We'd make a great team. Of course we'd have to move to some other town. The racket is shot here. How does Miami strike you?"

"My dear Louise," I said. "I am a man of rigid moral fiber. I would not for a moment consider—"

"It's perfectly safe. Even when you're found out, nobody ever takes it to the police. It's hush-hush all around because everybody's got a finger in the pie."

"That is not the question—"

"It's profitable. Very profitable. Did you know that two weeks ago I sold a Matisse to Langley for nearly—"

I held up a hand. "Langley? Who's Langley?"

"He's that art dealer on Jefferson Avenue."

I closed my eyes. But of course. Here I had assumed that McQuigg-ley, Appleby, Hanson, and Brinkmann represented all of the art dealers O'Brien had tried to blackmail. Why couldn't there have been more who were not necessarily privy to McQuiggley's group?

"How many dealers did you sell your paintings to?" I asked.

She thought for a moment. "Five. McQuiggley, Appleby, Hanson, Brinkmann, and Langley."I smiled. "Would you by any chance happen to know if Langley drives a light-colored late-model Lincoln Continental?"

"Why, yes. He once drove O'Brien and me to an exhibition." She stopped her eyes widening a bit. "Oh. The newspaper said O'Brien was run down by a light-colored late-model Lincoln Continental, didn't it?"

Exactly," I said. "Langley is our murderer." I went to the phone.

"Hold it," Louise said. What do you think you're doing?"

"I'm phoning the police. I'll wager that in Langley's garage they will find a light-colored late-model Lincoln Continental with a badly damaged fender or hood or both. And by comparing the paint chips undoubtedly found on O'Brien's clothes with the paint of the Lincoln Continental, they will unquestionably find that they match."

"So they match," Louise said. "But I still don't think you've got enough evidence to sustain a murder charge. If he admits to anything at all, it will be simply hit-and-run. And if he is convicted of that, what do you think will happen to him? He is an upstanding member of the community with some degree of money and an unblemished past. At the worst he will be given a year's probation and his driver's license will be suspended for thirty days."

I brooded on that darkly. Here I uncover a murder most foul and the murderer faces nothing more than the possibility of having his driver's license suspended for thirty days. Was it worth the trouble?

I sighed and put down the phone.

"Now, now," Louise said, "don't take it so hard. You cant expect justice to triumph all the time." She led me to the couch. "Sit down and we can talk some more about my proposition.

I am utterly incorruptible and I knew that I could not be swayed. However—in the interest of open-mindedness I thought I ought to give her the opportunity to exercise her logic, her persuasion, or any possible wiles she could think of to tempt me to join her in her nefarious activities.

The late movie featured *The Beast with Four Fingers*, which we watched now and then.

Cardula to the Rescue

Half a block ahead of me. the masked man sprang from the shadow of a public telephone booth and pounced upon the woman's handbag.

She clung desperately to its straps, thereby initiating a grim tug-of-war.

Even at this late hour, there were perhaps a half a dozen pedestrians within aiding distance, but they quickly turned their faces and scuttled away.

I sighed. People simply do not want to become involved any more.

I dashed forward and grasped the hoodlum's right wrist with sufficient firmness to rearrange the bones of his carpus. He shrieked, of course, and released the handbag. I then lifted him high overhead and tossed him some thirty feet onto a metal trash container at the curb. It collapsed under his weight and he lay inert among the ruins of metal, paper napkins, and old newspapers.

I turned to the woman, who was approximately in her middle-twenies and had dark hair and violet eyes.

"Madam," I said, "I trust that you are not injured?"

Her eyes were still wide. "I don't think so."

I indicated the phone booth. "I shall summon the police immediately."

Her eyes flickered. "I don't think that's really necessary. I mean, there was no harm done. After all, he didn't get the purse. Why bring the police into this?"

I noted the initials E.W. on the brooch she wore. "Madam, you are indeed generous-hearted. However, the odds are that this scoundrel has snatched dozens of purses and will continue to snatch more until some public-spirited citizen, such as yourself, sees that he is put behind bars by testifying against him."

I spied the lights of a police cruiser down the block and waved.

"What the hell are you doing?" she demanded.

"Flagging down a squad car."

She glared. "Why don't you mind your own damn business." Then she turned and disappeared into a dark alley between two buildings.

I blinked and then moved to the still-unconscious man amidst the debris. I pulled the nylon stocking from his head. He seemed to be in his middle thirties.

The squad car drew up to the curb and two officers got out. They su rveyed the situation and one of them addressed me. "What happened?"

I explained.

He looked about. "I don't see no lady."

I cleared my throat. "She seems to have disappeared."

He studied the unconscious purse snatcher. "I don't see him wearing no stocking over his head."

"I took it off. It must be somewhere in that rubbish."

He sighed.

"Mister, you're in big trouble. That trash container is city property and they don't come cheap."

The second officer walked back to the car to call an ambulance.

The first officer continued to eye me suspiciously. "All I see here is one man standing and another on his back. I don't see no lady or no stocking mask. What's the real story? I think maybe we'd better take you down to headquarters until we get this straightened out."

"Officer," I said, "I am a licensed and bonded private detective. Cardula is my name. " I reached for one of my cards and found myself staring into the barrel of his quickly drawn service revolver.

"Don't try nothing," he snapped. "Hands on the top of your head."

I did as directed and he proceeded to search me, but found no weapon. "Put your hands behind you."

I felt—and heard—handcuffs being snapped upon my wrists. "Now see here," I said, "This is absolutely ridiculous."

He shrugged. "So it's ridiculous. In which case your lawyer should be able to get you out in the morning."

Morning? That would never do.

I waited meekly until the arrival of the ambulance diverted his attention and then I broke away and dashed for the aperture into which the woman had disappeared.

In the darkness, I quickly shed the handcuffs and took refuge in a blind window high up on the building wall.

Below me the two officers dashed into the alleyway, their guns drawn and their flashlight beams playing about.

One of them picked up the handcuffs. "How the hell did he get out of these? They're still locked."

They continued down the passage to its other end and disappeared around the corner.

I quickly departed from the scene and went back to my office.

"Of course it's strange, Janos. Here I try to do my citizenly duty and I'm seized by the police."

"I mean that it is most unusual for a purse snatcher to be masked."

We entered our vehicle and Janos began driving. "What would a young woman be doing wandering around downtown at nearly four in the morning?" he wondered. "You don't suppose that she was a. . ."

"No," I said. "She looked quite respectable. Though to tell you the truth, Janos, I don't suppose that these days that is a criterion at all." I watched cross traffic as we stopped at a corner. "Janos, did you know that I can now distinguish between blood types A and B simply by the way they walk? I am quite certain she was a B."

Janos made a turn towards the freeway. "And how did your investigation of Mr. Decker go?"

"Fine," I said. "Just as Mrs. Decker suspected, her husband did not leave town on a business trip. He simply took his suitcase to the apartment of a Miss Leslie Schwendtke and he was still there when I broke off my surveillance at three-thirty this morning."

I live in a quite large Victorian mansion situated some thirty miles from the city in a comfortably desolate countryside. When we arrived home, I went directly downstairs to my quarters. I read a bit— stopping at ten minutes before sunrise—and then went to bed.

The next evening, Janos drove me directly to Miss Schwendtke's apartment and I resumed my surveillance.

At eight-thirty, Decker and Miss Schwendtke left the apartment for a motion picture theatre. I followed, of course. After the movie, they had a late dinner and a few drinks and then returned to the apartment. The lights went out shortly thereafter, but I remained on duty until 3:30 a.m., when I called it quits for the night and began my return to the office.

As I walked the street I'd used the night before, I thought I saw a familiar figure approaching.

Yes, as she came closer I recognized the same woman who had almost had her handbag snatched the previous morning.

She had nearly reached the point where the incident had occurred when a masked man sprang from the cover of a public telephone booth and grabbed for her handbag.

Once again she clung to it stubbornly and again the nearby pedestrians hurriedly disappeared.

As before, I swept down on the hoodlum. I grasped his larcenous right wrist and flung him through the air.

Too late, I realized that he was going to descend squarely on another metal trash container. It collapsed under him and he lay there senseless.

I turned to the woman and found her glaring at me.

"Damn you!" she snapped. And once again she turned and disappeared down the narrow passageway she had used the night before.

I watched her departure, shrugged, went to the recumbent figure, and removed the stocking from his head.

I blinked. Really, this was too much! It was the same man who had attempted to snatch the woman's purse earlier. I put my hand to my forehead. Was I losing my mind? Had I somehow inadvertently passed through a time warp? Was I doomed to repeat this purse-snatching episode over and over again?

If I turned now, would I see a squad car approaching?

I turned. I saw lights on the roof of a car down the street. Was it a squad car? Or a taxi?

I didn't wait to find out. I rushed to the passageway just in time to see the young woman reach the opposite street and turn to the right.

I flew quickly after her, seeing her again when I reached the opposite street. I followed her, keeping half a block behind.

She walked two blocks and then entered a large apartment building. I watched her enter the elevator and the lights above the door indicated that she got off at the nineteenth floor.

I went to the bank of mail slots in the foyer and studied those in the 1900 series. One contained a last name beginning with the letter W, and that was a Richard Walker and Elizabeth Walker in 1903.

I took the elevator to the nineteenth floor and found door number 1903. I looked about for a suitable hiding place and discovered an unlocked utility closet. I returned to 1903, pressed the buzzer, and quickly retreated to the closet, leaving the door open a fraction of an inch.

Who would answer the door? Richard Walker? Or a servant, if he had one? No. I thought that at this hour of the morning—nearly four—the one who answered the door would most likely be the one who was still awake, and that should be the young woman I had been following.

I was correct.

She opened the door and peered up and down the hall. Frowning, she closed the door again. I heard the bolt being shot home.

At the office, Janos was waiting, and as we drove home I told him about the second purse-snatching incident.

He was thoughtful. "This assailant, he was masked again?"

I nodded.

Janos sighed. "We have here a number of coincidences. First, there is the coincidence of your being at the same point, at the same time, two nights in a row."

"That isn't a genuine coincidence, Janos. I was watching the Schwendtke apartment. I quit at my usual time in such a case, and took the shortest route back to the office."

Janos frowned. "But then we have the coincidence of your tossing that man upon a trash container two successive nights."

"That also isn't as much of a coincidence as it first appears, Janos. When one throws anything one instinctively or unconsciously aims at something—a tree, a rock, a tin can. The trash container was simply the nearest logical target."

Janos pursued the point. "This trash container, sir. Was it the same trash can as last night?"

I pondered. "No, Janos, now that I remember it, there were two trash containers at the curb some fifty feet apart. Last night I destroyed one and tonight the other."

Janos was greatly relieved. "For a moment I had fears that you might have broken through a time warp and were doomed to repeat this episode over and over again. However—if I remember the rules for such situations correctly—it would have had to be the same trash can both nights."

Janos increased his speed on the freeway. "But we are still faced with the coincidence of this woman being on the street at the same early hour twice in succession and twice having someone trying to steal her handbag. And both attempts, apparently, by the same man."

"Janos," I said, "I could have sworn that he was a hospital case the first time I threw him through the air. I was at least positive that his right wrist would have to be put into a cast. Yet the very next night he reappears, hale and hearty."

Janos brightened. "I believe I have the answer to that conundrum sir. This was not one and the same person twice, but two different people who happened to be twins. Or possibly two of triplets, or quadruplets or quintuplets."

I agreed.

"You're right, Janos. Tomorrow I'll be at the same place at the same time to see if we are dealing with twins, triplets, or whatever."

I began the next evening, however, by resuming my surveillance of Miss Schwendtke's apartment. At ten, Decker left alone, carrying his suitcase.

He found a taxi downstairs and I followed as it drove him back to his own residence and, possibly, the arms of his wife.

I returned to my office, typed a report to Mrs. Decker, and, along with my bill, mailed it to her.

I spent the next few hours waiting for new clients—of which there were none. Finally at three A.M., I decided that instead of waiting for the Walker woman at her usual place, I might just as well begin the episode by following her from her apartment.

It was fortunate that I did, because when she came out of the building at three-thirty, she turned instead in a new direction.

She again carried the large handbag, however, and this time she stopped at the lighted display window of a bookstore. She appeared to be studying the book jackets, but now and then she glanced covertly up and down the almost deserted street.

Finally, she turned and went quickly to the metal trash container at the curb. Opening her handbag, she pulled out a large brown package and pushed it through the swinging top. Then she walked briskly away without looking back.

I frowned. Trash containers seemed to play an inordinately large part in this case.

My eye caught a movement down the block. A tall man carrying a briefcase stepped onto the sidewalk from the darkness of a doorway where he had evidently been lurking.

He approached the trash container, reached inside, and groped about until he pulled out the brown package. He quickly slipped it into his briefcase and departed.

I followed as he turned down a side street and slipped into an automobile parked at the curb.

He drove for some twenty minutes, turning constantly and doubling back in an obvious effort to throw off anyone who might be following him. Finally, he headed for the industrial valley of the city and stopped in front of a large, grimy warehouse.

After he entered the building, I myself found an opening through which I could slip.

The warehouse appeared to be filled to the rafters with bales of paper pulp.

From the advantage of height, I watched the tall man move down an aisle toward a corner which was separated from the rest of the building by eight-foot partitions.

I looked down into the enclosed space and saw two battered desks, some filing cabinets, and several chairs.

And tied securely to one of the latter was a man of about fifty, graying at the temples.

A heavy man wearing a gun in a shoulder holster greeted the tall man. "Well, Maxie, how did it go this time?"

Maxie patted the briefcase. "Like clockwork, Pete." He removed the package, tore off the paper cover, and poured bundles of currency onto one of the desks.

While they counted the packs of bills, I put two and two together.

Obviously this was a kidnapping. The man tied to the chair bore a certain resemblance to the woman in apartment 1903, and I deduced that he was probably her father.

He had been kidnapped and a ransom had been demanded.

Elizabeth Walker had left her apartment with instructions to deposit the money in a certain trash container on a downtown street.

But two unexpected things had happened. One, the purse snatcher had made an appearance, and, two, so had I. And in the ensuing action I had destroyed the very trash container into which she was to deposit the ransom money.

She had had no recourse but to return to her apartment and await further instructions from the kidnappers.

The tall kidnapper, Maxie, had probably been watching from a doorway and seen the incident. And acting on the wholly logical assumption that the purse-snatching could not reoccur in a hundred years, he had phoned her again and instructed her to repeat the errand the next morning, this time dropping the package into a trash container further down the street.

But once again history had repeated itself and another trash container had been obliterated.

Maxie, however, was not one to give up on trash containers, and a third time he directed her to another location. This time the transaction had gone off without a hitch.

Below me, they finished counting the money.

"Well, Pete," Maxie said, "it's all there. We had the damndest time but it worked."

Pete seemed to study him. "I been thinking things over, Maxie, amd I just don't believe it."

"Don't believe what?"

"This story you brung me twice about the purse-snatcher and the gent in black clothes who tosses him like a rag doll thirty feet or more onto trash cans."

"I know it's crazy, Pete, but it happened."

Pete eased his gun from the holster. "No, Maxie. I'll tell you what really happened. The first time you picked up the money all right, but you hid it somewhere and come to me with the story about the purse snatching. And then when you phoned the Walker dame again, you told her that the fifty grand was nice but that we wanted another fifty before we'd let her old man go."

"You got it all wrong, Pete."

Pete shook his head. "And the first time went so good, that you figured why not try it just once more. So you hid the second fifty grant too and came back to me with the same story you used the first time."

"Pete, I swear..."

"So you call the dame a third time, and once again she comes up with another fifty grand. But now you figure you can't pull the same deal any more, so you finally bring the money here." Pete glowered. "I say that you got a hundred grand packed away somewhere and now you even got the nerve to expect to get half of this last fifty thousand. In short, Maxie, you wind up with a hundred and twenty-five thousand, and I get a lousy twenty-five. Now somehow that don't seem to me to be fair." The automatic moved ominously.

Maxie paled and quickly held up a hand.

"All right, Pete, all right. So that's the way it went. But if you kill me, the money's lost." He licked his lips. "I'll show you where all of it is, just don't, don't . . ."

I nodded admiringly. Fast thinking on the part of Maxie. To continue claiming innocence would simply have led to his immediate death. But by confessing to a double-cross of which he was not guilty, he not only spared his life for the precious moment, but also gained time and the possibility of turning the tables later.

However, I thought that it was about time for action on my part. I left my rafter and dropped down to the cement floor directly in front of Pete.

He swore with surprise at the suddenness of my appearance and pulled the trigger of the automatic, the bullet ricocheting off my mesosternum.

I flicked the weapon from his hand and then dealt him a side-handed blow which rendered him distinterested and oblivious to all further proceedings.

In the meantime, Maxie had broken a chair over my head. I turned on him and heaved him high over the partition walls. He disappeared from my sight and landed somewhere in the warehouse proper with a satisfactory crunch.

I untied Walker and used the desk phone to call the police.

Walker was still wide-eyed. "You must be wearing a bulletproof vest."

I glanced at my watch. I could not wait for the police to arrive. They would insist on detaining me for questioning and that wouldn't do, this close to daylight.

"Who are you?" Walker asked.

I smiled sparingly. "At the moment I prefer to work with a certain degree of anonymity."

"But you deserve a reward."

Reward? Well, perhaps something, I thought. After all, I had put in some time on this job, authorized or not. And my suit and shirt had been ruined by that bullet.

Perhaps he could slip me a few hundred from the ransom money? But no. He would need all of it for evidence when the police arrived.

I consulted my watch again. "I'm sorry, but I cannot remain a moment longer. However, I shall get in touch with you again. Perhaps tomorrow evening."

When I left, I passed Maxie senseless upon the remains of a metal trash container.

I frowned. Now that was a coincidence.

I arrived at my office to find a worried Janos. We wasted no time reaching the minibus and arrived home three minutes before sunrise.

At sunset later in the day, Janos drove me to the Walkers' apartment building.

On the nineteenth floor, I pressed the buzzer at door 1903.

Elizabeth Walker answered the door. Her eyes widened. "Good heavens, it's you again!"

Walker came to my rescue. "Elizabeth, this is the man I was telling you about."

She allowed me to enter, but with some reluctance.

The Walker quarters were large and it was obvious from their furnishings that they had enough money to be worth kidnapping.

A middle-aged, sullen-faced woman in a cloth coat appeared from one of the side doors. "I'll be back about nine."

When she was gone, Walker said, "That was Maggie. She's a bit surly, but live-in servants are hard to find these days." He turned to his daughter. "Where is she going?"

"To the hospital to see her brothers. You remember them, don't you? They pick up Maggie every once in a while to take her to a movie or something."

Walker nodded. "Oh, yes. The twins."

"It's the strangest coincidence," Elizabeth said. "First, one of them had some kind of an accident and broke his right wrist and some rib. And the very next day exactly the same thing happened to the other twin. Maggie's tight-lipped about the whole thing and I probably wouldn't know about the accidents at all except that she was out both times when the hospital called."

I had, of course, been listening with a great deal of attention. "When you went out to deliver the ransom money, did Maggie know why you were going out and where?"

Elizabeth nodded. "After all, she was in on the ground floor as far the kidnapping was concerned. When she went to answer the door the two kidnappers forced their way into the apartment."

In on the ground floor? Was she a part of the kidnapping conspiracy? No, I didn't think so. Pete had spoken of a fifty-fifty split. There had been no mention of Maggie or her brothers.

Nevertheless, Maggie must have seen the opportunity to profit from the kidnapping herself. She had dispatched one of her brothers to the point where the kidnap money was to be delivered. He was to snatch Elizabeth's handbag and Maggie and her brothers would be fifty thousand dollars happier.

But that attempt had failed and so had the second. I wondered if there would have been a third try if Maggie's brothers had been triplets.

I sat down and proceeded to tell the Walkers why they should begin looking for a replacement for Maggie.

Cardula and the Kleptomaniac

It was a beautiful evening—full moon, cloudless sky, and no head-winds. I would have preferred to fly, but my client, Diana Weatherly, insisted upon driving me in her car.

"What was the size of the stone?" I asked.

"About fifteen carats."

"Valuable, of course?"

My dark-haired, violet-eyed client smiled. "Mr. Cardula, I don't believe that it could be replaced for under fifty dollars."

I pondered the point. "A fifteen-carat diamond pendant worth only fifty dollars?"

She explained. "The stone wasn't a genuine diamond. It was glass or paste, or plastic, or whatever they make those things out of these days."

"Hmm," I said intelligently. "Then the stolen stone was only a copy of the original pendant?"

"It wasn't a copy of anything. It was an original in itself."

I nodded. "Now let me reprise. Last night someone crept into your bedroom while you were asleep and stole this pendant?"

"Yes. I was waiting there in the semi-darkness to see who would steal it, but somehow I simply conked off to sleep instead."

"So this was all in the nature of a trap? You deliberately placed the pendant in an obvious spot in your bedroom and then pretended to fall to sleep? Unfortunately, your pretense turned into reality and you dozed off while the thief went about his work?"

She confirmed. "I just can't understand falling asleep like that. I mean, one would have thought that the excitement of the wait would have kept me awake and alert, but I believe I fell asleep almost as soon as my head hit the pillow. As a matter of fact, I slept until almost noon today and was still sleepy when I got up."

I rubbed my lean jaw. "It is my suspicion that you might have been drugged. Did you have a nightcap or something of that nature before you retired?"

"Well, it's a big weekend party and everybody drinks. I suppose any-body could have slipped something into one of my martinis."

"And this morning, when you discovered that your pendant was missing, you immediately raised the alarm?"

"Certainly not. We simply don't do things like that in my circle, not for a piece of fake jewelry. The only people who know that the pendant is missing are me, the thief, and you."

"Is any one of your guests in financial trouble?"

"Not as far as I know. We're all rather well off."

"But one can never tell, can one? What I am getting at is perhaps one of your guests, badly in need of money, hoped to realign fortune by stealing and selling a stone which he assumed was hundreds of thousands."

She shook her head. "Oh, no. That won't do as a motive here at all. You see, everybody—or at least the four specific persons with whom we are concerned—knew that the stone wasn't genuine because I told them so. The thief never would have stolen the pendant if he thought it was at all valuable."

I frowned at the atrocious green cufflinks I was wearing while I waited for clarification.

"The only respect in which I did lie," she said, "was to tell them that I regarded the pendant as a sort of good luck charm and was quite proud of it."

I drew my eyes away from the cufflinks. "Each of your guests—or at least a particular four—knew that the pendant was of no real monetary value and yet one of these four could not resist stealing it during the night? And further, you expected that the attempt would be made?"

She smiled sweetly. "I was not one hundred percent positive, but I did think there was a strong possibility."

My client had come to my office at a few minutes after nine this evening with the green cufflinks.

Now she said, "You see, one of those four I mentioned is a kleptomaniac. Or at least I think that he—or she—could be classified as such." She sighed. "It all started years and years ago. We grew up in the same neighborhood, went to the same schools, moved in the same social circles. We all live on Jefferson Point. You've heard of it, of course?"

Even I, a relative stranger to the area, had. Jefferson Point was an enclave of sorts, a colony of the wealthy beyond the suburbs of those who were simply well-to-do.

Diana took the freeway turnoff. "As I said, it began years and years ago. At parties and things like that. Quite often something would turn up missing—some little thing that was inexpensive, but personal. A comb, or a lipstick, a Mickey Mouse watch."

"Those things were stolen just from you?"

"Oh. no. The thief played no favorites. He took from anybody."

"No one ever took the matter to the police?"

"Of course not. He—or she—never stole anything of real value. And actually, most of the time the victim assumed that he or she had simply misplaced or lost the article and that it would turn up after a while, but it never did." She was thoughtful. "The thief was very careful and clever. Besides me, I don't think that there are more than two or three people in our circle who even suspect that there might be a kleptomaniac among us."

"It strikes me that stealing a pendant from your dresser during the night is not being very clever. Surely you would realize immediately that the object had been stolen, not misplaced."

"Yes, but the thief would count on me to suspect one of the ser-. vants. It is unthought of for any hostess on Jefferson Point to believe one of her guests capable of stealing a trinket."

"When did you first suspect that there was a kleptomaniac on Jefferson Point?"

"It was just after my blue rat-tail comb disappeared at the Emerson party two years ago. I was positive that I hadn't lost or misplaced it. Then I began to think about all of the other things that I and others had 'lost' during all those years, and it suddenly occurred to me that they might not have been lost at all."

"And so you began looking for the thief?"

"Yes. At first, of course, I had to deal with dozens and dozens of suspects. But then, by cross-checking who was at whose party when: something disappeared, I eventually narrowed down my list to four people."

"Did you mention to anyone that you were looking for the thief?"

"Of course not. Word would eventually have gotten to him, and he might have stopped stealing altogether, and I was dreadfully curious about who he might be."

"But now you seem to have decided to give up detecting for yourself and you have hired me, a professional."

"Yes, Mr. Cardula. Last night I failed and I think that baiting another trap tonight and expecting results would be just too optimistic. I doubt very much if the thief would steal from me on consecutive nights. And besides, my four suspects all leave tomorrow morning for their various jobs and things and there's no telling when I might get them all under the same roof again. Albert's in the Army and his leave is ending, Imogene has those boutiques she's opened in Chicago to keep her busy, Herbert has his medical practice, and Agnes spends most of her time following the sun." She took her eyes off the road for a moment to look at me. "That's where you and the cufflinks come in."

In my office she had presented me with the cufflinks. They were the most garish and obviously inexpensive set I had ever worn—or seen, for that matter. But they were, I will admit, attention getting.

"Do you think that your kleptomaniac will steal from a total stranger?"

"I don't see why not. He seems to have been completely indiscriminate in his victims."

I watched her. "Last night, if you had not fallen asleep and you had caught your kleptomaniac in the act, what would you have done?"

Her eyes flickered for a moment. "Why absolutely nothing. I would just have let him—or her—take the pendant while I pretended to be asleep. It is just to satisfy my curiosity that I want to find out who he is."

"And what am I expected to do when I see who the culprit is? Shall I pounce upon him?"

"Nothing of the sort," she said firmly. "Let him steal the damn cuflinks. I just want you to identify him to me immediately."

We drove along winding tree-lined blacktop until Diana finally turned into one of the estate lanes. She followed it and stopped before a large and well-lighted mansion. I gazed dubiously at the dozen or so cars parked in the driveway. "Just how many weekend guests do you have?"

"Twenty-three. However, we are concerned with only four of them. I wanted the thief to feel safe, secure, and daring in a herd, so to speak."

We got out of the car. "This is my parents' home," she said. "But they're in Europe at the moment and this is my bash. I doubt very much if anybody's missed me."

She stopped for a moment and then said, "Ah, what luck. Here are two of our suspects now. Albert and Imogene."

She led me to the side terrace and introduced me as a friend from Europe.

Albert Spurrier wore an immaculate Army uniform with a major's gold oak leaves. There were rows of ribbons and awards running across the left side of his jacket. He was perhaps six feet tall and could have been described as ruddy, one of my favorite colors.

"Albert used to be a Boy Scout," Diana said. "He earned every single award and badge they had to offer."

Albert nodded happily. "Only been done once before, you know, and I still am a scout, Diana. The leader of Troop 196 at the post."

"As you can see," Diana said, "Albert is quite a brave man. He has any number of combat awards."

Albert sighed. "That's the one part of the Army I dislike."

Diana smiled. "Albert is basically a pacifist."

He agreed. "Almost, Diana. I hate war, but I was drafted, faced up to my duty to my country, and went off as a private. Then I discovered that I liked the Army. Not war, mind you, but the regular routine of peacetime Army life that drives most other men out of their minds. So I managed to get an appointment to West Point and here I am today." He shook his head sadly. "War itself is so disorderly. Smashing things. It revolts the architectural and human ecologist in me. But the peacetime Army is quite another thing. To be frank about it, I love accumulating awards and badges and ribbons, though not combat stars. Or wounds, for that matter." He indicated a number of items on his chest. "I'm a qualified parachutist, shoot expertly with any weapon, and have just completed a ranger course. In September I'm off to helicopter school. They give the neatest badges. Real collector's items."

Imogene McCarthy had been listening patiently. She had auburn hair and was rather tall. She regarded me with some interest. "You have the most charming accent."

I bristled slightly. "Madam, I am positive that I do not have an accent."

"Well, you look as though you have an accent."

"Imogene collects elephants," Diana said. "Not the real live ones, of course. Those little china and plastic and glass ones."

"China only, dear," Imogene corrected. "That puts a sensible boundary on the whole damn project. "

"Imogene has a whole room at home devoted to shelves of china elephants," Albert said.

Imogene smiled patiently. "I started collecting when I was twelve. After two years, I'd completely lost interest in them, but by then it was too late. I already had two hundred elephants and had established a reputation. People still keep sending me elephants whenever they travel. From Bangladesh, Madagascar, Monaco. I personally haven't been in that room for ten years. But my parents tell me I am now the proud owner of almost a thousand china elephants and the end is still not in sight."

Diana Weatherly now directed our attention to the cufflinks I was wearing. "Why Mr. Cardula, I hadn't noticed those cufflinks before. How very extraordinary and rococo. I suppose they are ancient and priceless heirlooms?"

I regarded the horrible things with heroic fondness. "Why, no. As a matter of fact they are just green glass. However, I do treasure them for other reasons. They were given to me by an old gypsy woman with the exhortation that if I wore them, they would ward off evil. She added that once a month would be quite sufficient."

Since I do not drink—certainly not alcohol—and thus could not be drugged, I thought I would add something of my own to our trap. I politely covered a yawn. "I have just finished a tedious bit of traveling. I'll probably sleep like a log tonight. And once I get to sleep, nothing short of a cannon can wake me."

Diana began the process of moving me away. "I've got to introduce Mr. Cardula to a few other people. I hope the two of you are finding something to talk about?"

Albert nodded. "Actually, Imogene and I haven't seen each other since Roger's funeral."

Diana took my arm and we moved away. "Imogene was my dearest friend in school. But I must add that when I was about thirteen, I 'lost' a little bracelet that had four tiny little elephants dangling from it."

We entered the house and she indicated a tall dark man with a Mephistophelian beard at the other end of the room. "Dr. Herbert P. Jonas."

"And what does he collect?" I asked.

"Heartbeats," Diana said.

We edged through the guests until we reached the doctor.

"I was just telling Mr. Cardula about your record collection, Herb," Diana said and turned back to me. "Herb collects heartbeats. On tape, wire, records, and so forth. He has healthy heartbeats, morbid heartbeats, and sad heartbeats, happy heartbeats. You name a heart disease and he'll have a record of that one pounding away—ordinary hearts, extraordinary hearts, hearts of the famous. He has the heartbeat of Calvin Coolidge."

Dr. Jonas shrugged. "Actually, the sound quality is terrible. But the record has been certified as authentic." He studied me. "I am always on the lookout for unusual heartbeats. You wouldn't by any chance be a collector's item?"

"No," I said firmly. "My heart is quite normal. I'll stake my life on that." I winced slightly.

Diana discovered my cufflinks and bubbled, "I've been wanting to comment on what striking cufflinks you have, Mr. Cardula. A family heirloom, perhaps? Quite valuable, I suppose?"

I went through my routine for the benefit of Dr. Jonas, our third suspect.

Diana's eyes flitted about the room and finally settled upon another individual. "There's Agnes. I've simply got to have you meet her."

We left Dr. Jonas and threaded our way toward Agnes.

"Agnes has just gotten rid of her fourth husband. Three of the collection were tennis pros. I think she's gone back to her maiden name, which is Williams."

Agnes Williams was a striking blonde with no disappointing proportions and one had the feeling that she was tanned from crown to toe without interruptions. She appeared to be in deep conversation with a tall young man, also thoroughly tanned, whose first name proved to be Cedric.

Diana introduced us and after we successfully passed through our cufflink routine she said, "How is your tennis, Agnes?"

Agnes laughed lightly. "I've given it up. It just isn't my game." She shook her head sadly. "You know, Diana, times have changed so dreadfully that two of my ex-husbands are collecting alimony from me. They convinced the judge that they had the right to be maintained in the style of life to which I had accustomed them."

A small, happy smile crept into Cedric's face.

Diana regarded Cedric. "Cedric doesn't play tennis?"

"Absolutely not," Agnes said. "He has no use for the game. He's the golf pro over at the Nagawanah Country Club."

Agnes turned her critical attention to me. "You should get out in the sun more, Mr. Cardula. Get yourself a healthy tan."

"No," I said. "I am allergic."

She nodded sympathetically. "Why not try a sun lamp instead?"

"I have trepidations concerning sun lamps. I do not know if a sun lamp's beam carries exactly the same properties as that of the sun itself. Suppose I turned on the switch and . . ." I sighed. "I simply cannot afford to experiment. One mistake and it is my last."

When Diana and I were alone again, she said, "Well, there's your cast of suspects. I don't suppose you know which one of them is our kleptomaniac yet?"

"I rather suspect that I do. Though, of course, I may be mistaken."

Her eyes clouded in thought. "Was it something one of them said?"

"No, it was something you said. Tell me, at what time yesterday evening did you begin showing off the pendant and conveying your information concerning it?"

"At around ten. I wanted to make sure that all four of my suspects were coming before I set my trap and Imogene didn't get here until nearly that time."

There was a short silence and then she said, "Well, which one of them is the kleptomaniac?"

I smiled sparingly. "I cannot jeopardize the name of someone who may in fact prove to be innocent. We will set our little trap tonight and see if I am correct." I paused a moment. "Who was Roger?"

Her face seemed to freeze for a moment. "He was my brother."

"And he died?"

"Yes."

"An accident?"

"No." And it was obvious that she was not prepared to talk further on the subject. "Your room is on the second floor on the right at the end of the corridor."

I nodded. "And your suite?"

"Why do you need to know that?"

"Madam," I said, "when I discover who our kleptomaniac is, I intend to tell you immediately. I am not remaining for breakfast."

"My door is neaer down the corridor on the right-hand side next to the bust of Edgar Allan Poe," Diana said.

She left me to circulate among her guests and I edged my way back to Imogene McCarthy, the collector of elephants. When we were within speaking distance, he said, "Several people here have made reference to Roger's funeral. Roger was Diana's brother, wasn't he?"

Imogene nodded. "Yes. He was about a year older than she. They were inseparable. Roger was great fun, though he did tend to drink a little too much."

"It was a pity how he died," I said cleverly.

She agreed. "Yes."

There was a silence. I cleared my throat. "I've heard conflicting stories. "

She seemed surprised. "What's to conflict?"

There was a longer silence while she measured me. Then she smiled. "You haven't heard any conflicting stories at all, have you? As a matter of fact, you really don't know anything at all about Roger's death. You're just nosy and want to find out."

I found myself blushing, which is quite a strain.

She waved a hand. "Nosiness is nothing to be ashamed of. How else can we learn anything if we're not nosy? Roger was murdered. Somebody hit him over the head with one of my iron elephants."

Dutifully I said, "Iron elephants?"

"Yes. Just about two years ago, at my place. It's down the road about a mile." She took a drink from a passing servant's tray. "We had a weekend something like this one, with lots of guests."

She sipped the drink. "Well, came morning, Roger was found dead in his pajamas on the floor of his bedroom. He'd been struck over the head, as I say, with one of my iron elephants. "

"But I thought you collected only china . . ."

"I try to. But some people just can't get that distinction through their heads, so they send me other kinds too. Those damn plastic ones, or lead, or aluminum, or iron, or whatever. Well, I can't just toss them away. People would eventually learn about it and their feelings would be hurt. So Mother stores most of my non-china elephants in boxes, but she also distributes a few around the house as knickknacks. And there was an iron elephant on Roger's dresser—"

"But who killed him?"

"Nobody knows to this day. The police came and questioned everyone and took fingerprints. It was exciting, but they couldn't pin it on anyone. So they settled for the old intruder theory, because the French windows to the balcony were open."

She finished her drink. "You know the way it goes. The thief breaks into Roger's room. Roger wakes. The burglar panics and smashes Roger over the head with the nearest thing available."

"Was anything missing?"

"Roger's wallet was still on the dresser and it had about two hundred dollars in it, according to the police. They think that Roger woke before the burglar got to the wallet. And after killing Roger the intruder had nothing but escape on his mind."

"Are you satisfied with that theory?"

"Personally, I think that one of the guests did it, but I haven't the faintest suspicion who."

"Roger's sister was one of your guests?"

"Yes, poor dear. Of course it quite devastated her."

I casually exhibited my cufflinks again and stifled another yawn. "I hope it isn't impolite to leave the party, but I simply must go to my room and get some sleep. I'm dead tired. Once my head hits the pillow I sleep like a log."

"I know, " Imogene said.

I made my way to the second floor and stopped at the door of Diana's suite. I tried the doorknob and the door opened. I stepped inside. In the moonlight, I studied the room. There was the bed in which Diana must have been lying last night, and the dresser on which she had put the bait, her pendant.

She had intended to feign sleep and see who came to steal the pendant. She was going to do nothing to thwart or expose the thief. She just wanted to satisfy her curiosity.

Frankly, I didn't believe a word of it.

I moved to the nightstand on the right side of the bed and pulled open the top drawer.

Ah, yes.

I picked up and examined the revolver. It was a .48 Magnum, a weapon whose slug is touted as capable of destroying the engine block of an automobile.

I put the gun back into the drawer and left the room. I found my own bedroom and entered.

Should I read for a while? It could be hours before the guests settled in their rooms for the night. Probably my suspect would wait until two or three in the morning—an hour when he felt that everyone would be asleep—before he set about the task of stealing my cufflinks. On the other hand, he might be bolder and simply steal away from the party now and risk entering my bedroom. After all, I had quite thoroughly established that once I got to sleep it was impossible to wake me.

I really couldn't take any chances. I unsnapped my cufflinks and put them on the dresser. Then I took off my shoes and lay down on the bed, pulling the covers up to my chin.

Frankly, I should have read. It was hours before I heard the last guests finding their rooms and settling down for the night.

I continued to wait, frequently consulting my digital watch, and began to have doubts that my bait was to be taken.

Three A.M. passed. I most certainly would have to leave before four if I wanted to arrive home before sunrise.

My hearing is abnormally acute and so I caught the faint click of a door being opened somewhere down the hall. I waited, and soon distinguished the brush of shoes or slippers on the hall runner. The sounds came closer, then stopped just outside my door.

The moonlight provided sufficient light so that I could see the doorknob slowly turn. I closed my eyes to slits, and watched the door being pushed silently open. A dark figure appeared in the doorway and stood obviously listening.

I decided to breathe rather heavily. That would have to be sufficient. I refused to stoop to the indignity of a snore.

After a few more moments, my intruder appeared to be satisfied. The figure moved quickly to the dresser, scooped up the cufflinks, and darted out of the room. It was all over within a matter of seconds, during which time, however, I was clearly able to establish the identity of the kleptomaniac.

When the intruder was gone, I waited a few minutes and then put on my shoes. I went out to the small balcony outside my windows and circled the house.

Only two windows on the second floor of the wing were lighted.

In one of the rooms I saw the kleptomaniac, eyes gleaming, examining the cufflinks.

And in the other, Diana sat in her bed reading a book and glancing impatiently at her watch, obviously waiting for news concerning our kleptomaniac.

I tapped on the French windows.

She was startled, but when she saw it was me, she rose and unlocked them. She stared past me and frowned. "How did you get here? This balcony doesn't connect to yours."

"Never mind that," I said. "Suffice it to say that I am here."

She brightened immediately. "The trap worked? You know who the kleptomaniac is?"

I rubbed my jaw—happily noting the absence of the cufflinks. "Madam, why do you keep that revolver in your night stand?"

Her eyes went to the object of furniture in question. "How did you . . ." Then she shrugged. "For protection, of course."

"You purchased the weapon yourself?"

She shrugged again. "Yes."

I smiled. "No, madam, it is extremely doubtful that you bought that revolver yourself for yourself. Not a .48 Magnum. Women tend toward the traditional .22. Or possibly, in our liberated age, the bold .32. But a .48 Magnum? Never. Even if you went to a gun store fully primed to buy a .48 Magnum, any clerk worth his salt would succeed in directing you to a smaller caliber."

"So I didn't buy it myself," she said. "It used to belong to Roger. What difference does it make?"

"Madam, I was merely pursuing the point that if one lies about one thing one is likely to lie about others. Therefore, I submit that last night when you baited your trap it was not with the innocent intention of merely satisfying your curiosity as to the identity of the kleptomaniac. When the thief picked up that pendant, you premeditatedly intended to blast his engine block . . ." I regrouped. "You intended to blast the vitals from his body."

"Ridiculous," she said, avoiding my eyes. "Now who is the klepto?"

I continued. "And why would you want to destroy a relatively harmless kleptomaniac?" I permitted myself another small smile. "Because he is not a relatively harmless kleptomaniac. This individual has done something to you—or yours—which you feel merits his murder."

I regarded her penetratingly. "And this brings, to mind the death of your brother. It is my deduction that you suspect that the killer of your brother is also the neighborhood kleptomaniac. There was something about Roger's death that convinced you."

She was silent for thirty seconds and then decided to talk. "The ring. Roger's missing ring. He wore two rings. One of them was obviously worth thousands of dollars. The thief did not take it. The other was a class ring, just a silver ring with Roger's initials and the date his class graduated, 1971. I don't believe it was worth more than thirty dollars. But the thief took that." Her eyes met mine fiercely. "Don't you see? That night two years ago Roger had quite a bit to drink and the kleptomaniac counted upon Roger being in a deep sleep. But as he was removing the ring from Roger's finger, Roger woke up and recognized him. Or her. The kleptomaniac killed him rather than being unveiled to the world."

"Why didn't you tell the police about the missing ring?"

"Because at the time I didn't realize it was gone. I mean, just seeing his body like that blotted out everything else. It wasn't until weeks after his funeral that I realized the ring had been missing."

"But you still didn't go to the police with the information?"

"Frankly, by that time I had lost all confidence in the police. It seemed to me that the only way the killer would ever be uncovered was to find the kleptomaniac. But if they bungled that job too, they might frighten him into never stealing again and my last hope of catching him would disappear. No. I wanted him to think that he had gotten away with murder and keep stealing again and again until I finally tracked him down."

"Diana," I said, "has it ever occurred to you that the kleptomaniac and the murderer might not be one and the same person?"

"But the missing ring . . ."

I held up a hand. "The kleptomaniac might have stolen the ring while Roger was still alive and sleeping. And later, someone else—another guest or possibly even this suspected intruder—could have entered the room and killed Roger for another reason. Or possibly the killing was done first, and when the kleptomaniac entered the room on his own mission he was not deterred by the fact that Roger was dead."

She shook her head. "Something like that would be just too much of a coincidence. I mean, murder and kleptomania to the same man the same night."

I offered another possibility. "Suppose that after murdering Roger, the killer decided to put the blame on the kleptomaniac by also stealing Roger's ring. Unfortunately for him, nobody noticed that the ring was missing. "

Diana dissented again. "But if the killer went to the trouble of stealing the ring and nobody noticed it was missing, wouldn't he somehow call attention to the fact himself? Wouldn't he casually clear his throat and say something like 'By Jove, isn't Roger's class ring missing?' But no one did." She folded her arms. "All right, now who is our kleptomaniacal killer?"

I hesitated. "You still have no intention of taking the matter to the police?"

"With no tangible evidence that the kleptomaniac and the killer are the same? No, the only solution—the only justice—is for me to kill the killer myself."

"Diana, do you realize that if you do kill Roger's murderer you will undoubtedly go to prison for a long, long time?"

She squared her shoulders. "I don't care. Who is the kleptomaniac?"

I shook my head. "I haven't the slightest intention of telling you. Firstly, because I do not want to see you go to prison, and secondly, because the police might construe that I am an accessory to murder by providing the name of the victim."

She became demanding. "I'll give you ten thousand dollars for his name."

"No."

"Twenty thousand."

"No."

Eventually she reached the "I'll give you a blank check" stage, but I remained adamant.

She took a deep breath. "Very well. But you aren't the only private detective in the world. I'll hire another—as many as I need—until I find out who killed Roger."

I glanced at my watch. It was that time again. "I'm afraid I must bid you an immediate goodnight."

I left her in her room and walked down the corridor until I found the free night air and headed for home.

The next evening, when I rose, I shaved, showered, and proceeded to my office. I consulted the telephone book for the home address of my killer/kleptomaniac and wrote it in my notebook.

I waited until ten o'clock and then took off for Jefferson Point. Since I was not familiar with the region or its winding roads, I was forced to descend a number of times to consult directional signs and numbers before I finally found the house for which I was searching. I circumnavigated the building until I found lights in a second-floor bedroom. Inside, my kleptomaniac was in the process of unlocking a large suitcase on the bed. The lid sprang open.

I blinked.

The suitcase was filled to overflowing with bracelets, rings, combs, necklaces, baubles, and gewgaws of every sort. Evidently I had arrived at that hour of the evening when he gloated over the spoils.

I turned the knob of the French window and stepped softly into the room. I moved toward the killer, who remained completely unaware of my presence.

What motivated the kleptomania I could not guess—I am not a psychiatrist—but I did know that the future portended that Diana would eventually track down her brother's killer and in turn become a murderess and be sent to prison.

Hardly a proper ending for this case.

Yet Diana was quite right. Justice must be done, though it must be done with more expertise and anonymity.

I reached forward and tapped Dr. Herbert P. Jonas on the shoulder. He leaped into the air and when his feet touched the rug again, he was facing me, his eyes wide and wild.

I indicated the collection and clucked my tongue. "So you are the Jefferson Point kleptomaniac."

He stared at me. "Who the devil are you and how did you get in here?" And then he recognized me.

I nodded. "I am Cardula. Licensed and bonded private detective." I indicated the array again. "It is my duty to expose you to the world."

He ran his tongue over his lips. "Now just one moment, Mr. Cardula. Couldn't we come to some . . ."

I stayed his words. "No, Dr. Jonas. I am impossible to bribe into silence." I went to his bedside phone and picked it up. This put my back to him, though I did still have a fair view of him through the dresser mirror. I began dialing at random.

What *would he* do now? I wondered. I stopped dialing and pretended to be waiting for the connection to be made. Jonas's eyes darted madly about the room and then decided upon a heavy glass ashtray. He picked it up and advanced behind me, arms upraised.

Ah, I thought with some satisfaction, I had not said that I would expose him as a murderer. Merely a kleptomaniac. But he considered that quite a sufficient reason to kill me—just as, it was now obvious, he had killed Roger Weatherly.

I turned quickly, dropped the phone, and swiftly and efficiently snapped his neck.

A certain basic logic had led me to suspect him from the beginning. On the night her pendant had been stolen Diana had obviously been drugged. After all, one simply does not drop off to innocent sleep when one is waiting to kill someone.

And does your average soldier, or elephant or husband-collector carry about on his person for instant use knockout drops or sleeping powders? If lengthy premeditation to steal were involved, perhaps yes. However, none of the suspects even knew of the existence of Diana's pendant until ten o'clock that night.

And so that left Dr. Jonas, who, like all physicians, was never far from his black bag and its contents. Probably he had kept it in his car. And once determined to steal the pendant, he had simply gone outside, fetched the amount of sleeping potion he needed, and slipped it — into one of Diana's drinks.

I poured the contents of the suitcase out upon the bed. Yes, there were my cufflinks, hideously obvious even in that mélange. I rummaged through the collection until I found a silver ring bearing the initials R.W. and the date 1971. I sighed and put it back.

I carried the body of the now defunct Dr. Jonas out to the balcony and dropped it to the driveway below.

When daylight came, he would be discovered and the police would be called. They would investigate and come upon the bed strewn with its trinkets, the bizarreness of which would certainly get Jonas's demise a prominent place in the newspapers. The identification of various objects long thought lost by the residents of Jefferson Point would follow and the neighborhood kleptomaniac would finally be unmasked.

And the police? They would eventually assume that Dr. Jonas had gone out onto the balcony for a breath of fresh air or to admire the moonlight and that somehow he had tripped over the low railing and snapped his neck on the driveway below.

I stood on the balcony, looking down at the body.

What blood type was he, I wondered? A pos.? A neg.? B pos.? The hell with it. I wouldn't touch him again with a ten-foot pole.

I flew back to my office.

Cardula's Revenge

"It's that beast Van Jelsing again," Nadia said.

I raised an eyebrow. "By this time that man must certainly be in his hundreds."

She shook her head. "The original Van Jelsing is dead. This is his grandson, Professor Van Jelsing the Third. But he, too, shares the family obsession."

"Is he after anyone in particular this time?"

"I don't think so. Ostensibly he is here in America on a lecture tour, peddling his favorite subject. But no doubt he will also be sniffing around, just having him in the neighborhood sends shivers up and down my spine."

Nadia's eyes appraised my office, the furniture of which consisted of a desk, two chairs, a filing cabinet, and one typewriter. She was not very impressed. "My friends told me that you were now a private detective."

I nodded. "One must live. Everything I brought over from the old country eventually had to be pawned."

Nadia's smile was rather self-satisfied. "I invested everything I had in Xerox, at the very beginning. Now I live in Wurthington Hills."

Nadia had raven-black hair, an eye-catching pale complexion, and wore obviously expensive clothes. "Do you remember Yvette of Strasbourg?"

"Certainly In the old days she was frequently a weekend guest in the castle. She is a most talented pipe organist. What a magnificent left hand she has."

Nadia made a correction. "Had. Yvette will never play again."

"Van Jelsing?"

"Yes. And have you ever met little Nicco?"

"Of course, the world's leading authority on archaic Latin. It was his natal tongue, you know. Not little Nicco too?"

"Van Jelsing got to him in a wine-storage cavern just outside of Florence." Her thin strong fingers moved convulsively. "I would like to snap Van Jelsing's neck. Crack! Just like that."

And, given the opportunity, she could do it too. I myself had the strength of twenty. And she, perhaps that of thirteen or fourteen.

"Something has got to be done about that man," Nadia said. "But none of us can get near him. He always wears that damn collar around his neck."

Ah, yes. The Van Jelsing leather collar with its numerous cruciform inlays. It is worn under the shirt, and as long as a Van Jelsing, or anyone else for that matter, wears it, he is impregnable—as far as we are concerned.

"Somehow he's got to be caught when he's not wearing that collar," Nadia said. "And that is why I am here. I ask you to take this mission and I am willing to pay you handsomely."

I pondered. "Where is Van Jelsing now?"

"He's staying at Mamie Bellingham's place while he does a series of lectures at the university. Mamie has invited me over to meet him, of course, but I wouldn't dream of getting within a mile of that man."

"Mamie Bellingham?"

"Yes, she is my *dearest* friend. We are practically like sisters. I am jealous only of her ability to tan."

"Nadia," I said, "do you suppose you could wrangle me an invitation to her home?"

"As a matter of fact, she is having a bash over there this Saturday in Van Jelsing's honor. You won't need an invitation because there will be hundreds of people there and Mamie cannot possibly know them all. Just drop in. I am certain no one will try to evict you."

When Nadia was gone, I resumed thinking.

Even when hidden from the eye, the Van Jelsing collar still seemed to provide its wearer with a protective force field. I had, at one time while in a confrontation with Van Jelsing *grand-père*, considered attacking him at some non-traditional point, even going so far as to try the tip of a finger,

However, I found that I could not approach within ten feet of him without acute discomfort.

Ah, well, I would just have to wait patiently and seize any opportunity, should it present itself.

Early Saturday evening I dropped into a novelty store and purchased a false moustache—a rather formidable Hussar type—on the assumption that while Van Jelsing the Third had never seen me in the flesh, he might still recognize me from old portraits.

I had received directions from Nadia on how to find Mamie Bellingham's estate, and, as I approached the general area, I had no trouble in being specific. The Bellingham house was quite thoroughly lit up.

Once down in the garden, I straightened my tie and proceeded toward the house. When I entered the sizeable drawing room, I saw a circle gathered about someone to the far side of the room.

I heard a voice expounding.

"They have, during the course of the centuries, developed a certain ecological restraint. They no longer completely drain their victims, thereby encouraging overcrowding in their ranks and competition for the available food supply. Instead they now merely stop for a sip here and a sip there until their need is fulfilled."

One of his audience asked a question. "Why don't their victims raise the alarm?"

"Because the victims are subjected to a hypnotically induced amnesia. They remember nothing of what happened to them. In the morning they wake, feeling perhaps a bit worn and wondering if possibly they are coming down with the Russian flu."

I gradually inched my way forward until I was in a position to get a view of Professor Van Jelsing the Third. He appeared to be the very image of his grandfather, even to the steel-rimmed glasses and the aura of smug pedanticism.

An anxious female voice inquired, "Then they can at this very moment be among us?"

"Yes," Van Jelsing said. He held up a hand to dispel the murmuring. "However, I have a certain sixth sense about their presence and I assure you that there are none of them in this room at the moment."

If this was an example of his sixth sense, I wondered at the condition of his other five.

Van Jelsing smiled complacently. "There are means by which one can distinguish them, and, contrariwise, there are means by which you can undistinguish them."

Very properly, someone asked, "Undistinguish?"

Van Jelsing nodded and pointed a finger directly at me. "You, sir, could not possibly be one of them."

I was a bit taken aback. "And why not, sir?"

"Because you are wearing a moustache. They do not grow moustaches. I don't know why, but they do not."

Another voice spoke up. "If they know that you're hunting them, don't they try to strike back?"

"Ah, yes," Van Jelsing said happily. "They try. But I am invulnerable." He whisked off his string tie in a practiced manner and began to unbutton the top of his shirt.

I averted my eyes, pretending a consuming interest in the conclusion of my trouser crease.

There was a gasp from Van Jelsing's audience.

"You see," Van Jelsing said. "I wear this collar around my neck at all times. Except when I am taking a shower."

I blinked. Shower?

He closed the door. "However, I never take a shower except during daylight hours. You will notice that on this collar I have had my protecting symbol artistically reproduced twenty-four times. I do not believe in taking chances by leaving a blind spot anywhere."

Finally allowing a furtive look, I saw that Van Jelsing had rebuttoned his shirt.

Professor Van Jelsing the Third now proceeded to introduce the man at his side. "This is my nephew, Henrik Van Jelsing, my protégé. I have chosen him to carry on my work after I am gone. Unfortunately, all of my own children were daughters and none of them chose to follow in my footsteps."

Henrik Van Jelsing was a sturdy individual with straw-colored full hair and a firm, square chin, Holland-blue eyes, and he appeared to be in his early twenties. He nodded modestly. "Originally I was with my father in the gladiola- and tulip-farming business, but the professor convinced my parents that my future lay in other fields. However, in order that I would never forget my roots, on my departure, my mother presented me with a potted gladiola, which I carry always with me in my travels."

I withdrew from the crowd and found myself melancholically regarding the other guests.

One of them seemed a bit familiar.

He was a thin individual with a hairline moustache, rather handsome in his middle-aged way, and there seemed to be the debonair air of the civilized rogue about him.

And now I remembered. It had been Scotland. Lady McDonnely had been celebrating the reappearance of the Loch Ness Monster after a lapse. "It was several years and it was just about time too. The tourist trade had fallen and the locals were beginning to grumble." Yes, it had been quite a large party.

I frowned. But that wasn't the only time I had seen that man. There had been the Le Mans Grand Prix and the Contessa Stella's pre-race ball.

I studied him. His attention seemed to return periodically to a rather impressively built woman with glaringly red hair some dozen feet away.

Yes, I thought, that must be Mamie Bellingham. Nadia had described her to me.

Scotland, Le Mans, and now Mamie Bellingham's mansion?

I further refined the area of his attention. It was not Mamie Bellingham herself who drew his interest, it was the shimmering necklace around her neck.

That was it—the common denominator. A casket of Lady McDonnely's jewelry had been stolen on the night of the Loch Ness ball. It appeared that she had gone to bed drugged, for she slept until noon the next day. When she awakened, she discovered her jewelry missing. And the Contessa Stella. Her blue-white pendant, the Star of Bologna, had also disappeared during the night and she also had apparently been drugged.

I rubbed my chin and then gradually sidled my way toward the man until I was next to him. I didn't know his name, but I said, "Well, well, Mr. Devlin, how nice to see you again."

He regarded me politely. "I'm afraid you have me confused with someone else, sir."

I peered at him for a moment and then admitted my error. "Of course. I'm sorry, I could have sworn I saw you come into my shop with Mamie Bellingham last week when she brought her necklace for repair."

He was faintly interested. "Repair?"

"Yes, the clasp of her necklace was broken and she brought it to me."

"You are a jewelry repairman?"

I chuckled good-naturedly. "Good Jupiter, no. I merely see to these little things to keep my customers happy. I am the junior member of Espanger and Espanger. Perhaps you've heard of us? Last week we sold the Wamberly Sapphire to the Sheik of Imafret. It was one hundred and twelve carats, a beautiful stone."

His estimation of my social value rose. "I see you were able to repair the clasp on Mrs. Bellingham's necklace."

"Unfortunately, no. It was beyond repair and the replacement was of such a distinctive nature that I was forced to send out for it. It hasn't arrived yet."

He stared at Mrs. Bellingham. "What's holding up the necklace?"

I laughed lightly. "Oh, that necklace. It's just her copy. The original is still waiting in the safe at our establishment."

He snatched a drink from the tray of a passing waiter. "You mean to say that she's wearing paste? That isn't the real necklace?"

"Goodness, no! Isn't it amazing what can be done with plastic combinations these days?"

He downed the drink.

I smiled. "Yes, I do try to keep my customers happy by doing the little shopkeeper favors and they learn to depend upon me. I suppose that's why Mrs. Bellingham sent Van Jelsing to me this morning. One of the larger diamonds in his collar had fallen out and he wanted it re-cemented."

Devlin, or whoever he was, looked Van Jelsing's way with growing interest. "I thought all those sparkles were rhinestones. That's the tiniest dog collar I've ever seen."

"The whites are diamonds," I said. "None less than two carats. The blues are sapphires, and the reds, rubies. And, if I'm not mistaken, there is a touch of lapis lazuli here and there."

Having planted the seed, I now left him with something to think about and made my way to the second floor.

I removed my moustache. It had begun to irritate me tremendously.

I gingerly touched my upper lip. Yes, it was swollen and very likely red. Was I allergic to moustaches?

I found a place of concealment and proceeded to wait. How long was this party intended to last? I hoped not into the morning hours.

I was rather relieved when toward 1:00 A.M. I saw Van Jelsing and his nephew ascending the thickly carpeted stairs.

Van Jelsing yawned and seemed to be depending upon his nephew for some support. "I don't know when I've felt so sleepy. It could not have been the drinks. I had only two all evening. Perhaps I have still not adjusted to jetlag."

His nephew guided him to a door, where Van Jelsing turned. "I'll be all right, Henrik. I just need a little sleep. You go back downstairs and enjoy this party."

Van Jelsing disappeared behind his door and his nephew went back downstairs.

I followed.

It was a matter of perhaps half an hour before I saw Devlin moving silently up the stairway. Evidently he did not know which bedroom was Van Jelsing's, because he tried several doors before he found the right one.

He slipped into the room and in less than a minute he was out again, a smile on his face, patting his right hand jacket pocket.

I waited until he disappeared down the stairs and then descended from my perch. I flexed my fingers. Within the minute they would be around Van Jelsing's neck.

I opened his door and entered the room. I saw two beds. Evidently Van Jelsing and his protégé shared the huge bedroom.

And there lay Professor Van Jelsing, gently snoring. The first two buttons of his pajama top had been undone and his neck was now bereft of the Van Jelsing collar.

My eyes were diverted to the nightstand beside his nephew's bed. It supported a pot containing the sword-shaped leaves and the crimson blossom of a single gladiola.

I studied it for a full thirty seconds and then I moved it to the chair next to Van Jelsing's bed.

It was some eleven months later when Professor Van Jelsing came to my office again, his face familiarly haggard. "I am a nervous wreck. I just got out of Lisbon by the skin of my teeth. My plane was taxiing down to the runway when I looked out of a window and there was that idiot nephew of mine with his satchel, watching my plane and rubbing his jaw."

He sat down. "That man is absolutely relentless. You would think since he is a blood relative, he would spare me. Or at least pursue someone else. But no. I am hounded—Dublin, Oslo, Constantinople, Ulan Bator. No one here—am I safe?. I am haunted by visions of Henrik pursuing me, a hammer in one hand and that damn wooden—"

I commiserated. "He does seem to be quite persistent."

Van Jelsing nodded. "I still don't really know how it all happened. All I remember is that I woke in the middle of the night knowing that I had to get the hell out of Mrs. Bellingham's house before daylight and realizing that it was imperative that I find some of my own native soil. Luckily Henrik's stupid gladiola plant was on a chair next to my bed. I filled my tobacco pouch with some of the soil and departed. Even then I think I would have perished if you hadn't accidently bumped into me on the street and taken me in for the day."

He studied me for a moment, as though trying to remember something "Did you ever wear a moustache?" Then he shrugged. "No. We don't grow moustaches. I don't know why, but we don't." He sighed. "Thank Lucifer, I don't have to transport a bulky box every time I have to move, as it was in the old days. A tobacco pouch under my pillow seems to be sufficient."

I agreed. "Essentially it's the thought that counts."

He wiped his forehead. "I had thought of going down to New Orleans but I think the high humidity might be bad for my arthritis. I believe I'll try Las Vegas instead."

I approved. "I spent a pleasant six months there several years ago. I had a suite at the Desert Cacti Hotel."

"How are the rates?"

"Quite reasonable."

He looked a bit embarrassed. "What with all this traveling, I seem to have run a little short. You don't suppose that—"

"But of course." I went to my office safe and removed three thousand dollars from the contingency fund Nadia and a few of her wealthy recluses had raised and handed it to Van Jelsing.

He pocketed the money. "I'll pay this back someday."

"I'm certain you will. Do keep in touch."

Henrik was plainly unhappy. "I wish he would hold still. All I am trying to do is put his soul to rest, but he doesn't seem to appreciate it. Frankly, I hate all of this traveling. And it is so expensive."

"Are you perhaps getting low on funds?"

"Well, it is getting to that point again."

"I'll wire you a few thousand."

"That is very kind of you." There was a pause. "Once I have put Uncle to rest, I am giving up this whole business and returning to my gladiolas and tulips."

"But in the meantime, Henrik, hang in there." I smiled. "And good hunting."

The Return of Cardula

"Albert's last words were 'No snow.'"

I frowned thoughtfully. People do seem to babble the oddest things when they depart this world. Especially murder victims. "What were the weather conditions at the time of Albert's death?" I asked.

"The temperature was in the low seventies. You couldn't *buy* snow on a night like that."

Which reminded me. "Now be utterly honest with me, sir. In the vernacular of the underworld, snow often refers to drugs of one kind or another. Were you and Albert by any chance involved in drugs?" .

His expression indicated that he was clearly above that sort of thing. "We wouldn't touch anything that heavy. We were just ordinary thieves."

I had arrived at my office at nine P.M.

I closed the window against the night air, hung up my cape, and proceeded to unlock the door to my waiting room.

I found a client already seated there. I always leave the door between my waiting room and the hall unlocked. He seemed startled to see me. "Were you inside there all the time?"

I smiled economically. "Have you been out here long?"

"About twenty minutes."

He was a small man of middle years with blinking eyes and a nervous manner. He studied me dubiously, as people have a tendency to do when they first meet me. "Are you Cardula?"

"Yes." I showed him into my office and offered him a chair.

He sat down. "I finally couldn't stand it any longer. I decided that I ought to see a private detective and find out what could be done. I was going to go the first thing tomorrow morning, but when I looked up names in the phone book I saw that your display ad said Night Hours, so I decided to come here right away and get it over with." He hesitated. "Is a private eye something like a priest or a lawyer? I mean if you tell him something does he keep it to himself?"

"Sir, I assure you that anything you have to tell me will travel no further."

That satisfied him. "My name is Walter Pierce. I'd like you to solve a murder."

"Sir," I said, "I do not wish to discourage business, but the regular police possess the numbers, the expertise, and the communications needed to handle matters as grave as murder. Contrary to popular belief, private detectives rarely, if ever, deal with murder."

"But the police still haven't found the murderer, and I don't think they ever will."

"When did this murder occur?"

"About two months ago."

"And the victim?"

"Albert Marshall. Albert and me were partners. We were together for more than thirty years. In jail and out. Mostly in. We'd get caught together, serve time together, and get paroled together."

Naturally I wanted to hear more about that. "Jail?"

He nodded. "The fact of the matter is that Albert and me were thieves. Mostly burglary, but also whatever else came along. That's why we were at the ball park. Not to see the game—we never even read the sports pages of the newspapers—but to go through the locker rooms while the players were out on the field. You know, scoop up anything we could lay our hands on—watches, wallets, rings, anything that looked valuable."

"Wouldn't you expect to find somebody in the rooms watching the players' possessions?"

"Sometimes there'd be somebody there and sometimes not. Whenever we found anybody, we'd just pretend we were lost and walk out again."

He rubbed his jaw. "Well, this time we did things a little different because of the layout. There was this long low corridor, like a tunnel, under the stands leading to the locker rooms and it made a turn. If we both went in there and something happened that we didn't expect we could get trapped. So we decided that one of us would stay at the entrance, like a lookout, and the other would go inside and do the job. If anybody showed up while Albert was at work, I'd stall him long enough so Albert could finish up inside and get out of there."

Pierce sighed. "So I stood there and watched Albert disappear down the corridor. And two minutes later I saw Albert again—only this time he had one hand tight against his chest and he was staggering. He came back up to me, his eyes wide, and said, 'No snow.' Then he dropped dead at my feet.

"At first I thought it was a heart attack, but then I saw the hole in his chest. There wasn't much blood—just around the edges of the wound and on Albert's hand. What I figure happened is that somebody was there in the locker room, only Albert didn't know it. When he saw Albert going through the lockers collecting, this unknown person grabbed a gun and fired."

"Did you hear the shot?"

"No. Where I was standing the noise from the fans must have drowned it out. So there I was with Albert's body, but I couldn't go to the police because I hadn't reported to my parole officer for over a year and that could get me into a lot of trouble. So I just had to leave Albert lying there and let somebody else find his body."

Pierce shook his head sadly. "Albert was even smaller than I am and weighed ten pounds less. You could have said boo and Albert would have dropped everything and run like a rabbit. There wasn't no cause to shoot him."

Now I vaguely remembered reading a newspaper item about the body of a man being found in a corridor under the stands at the County Stadium. The police had speculated that he might have been the victim of a robbery attempt that went awry.

I reflected. "If Albert was shot by someone in the locker room, why didn't that person come forward and admit as much? I don't remember reading anything to that effect in the newspapers."

Pierce smiled thinly. "Nobody ever came forward. Whoever shot Albert wasn't too proud of what he'd done. Maybe because it was really murder. I was hoping the police would find him, but since that doesn't look likely anymore I decided to come to you and see if anything can be done about it."

"Whose locker room had Albert been rifling? The home team's or the visitors'?"

"The home team. If everything went right we were going to go through the visitors' next."

When Pierce left, I pondered. Who had killed Albert? A locker-room attendant? Or perhaps even a player who had lagged behind for some reason? A visit to the stadium might be in order.

I found the evening's newspaper in the waiting room and turned to the sports pages. Ah, good, there was a game tonight.

It was approximately four miles to the County Stadium—as the crow flies, so to speak—and when I arrived I descended to a dark spot behind the last seats in the upper grandstand.

I studied the playing field far below. Even with my ultra-keen eyesight I could barely distinguish the numbers on the backs of the players. Clearly I had to get a better view.

I strode down the ramp to the lower grandstand and then down the aisle to the box seats near the diamond. I found two empty seats and took one of them, which gave me an excellent close view of the players. I purchased a score card and settled down to observe. A beer vendor passed and I was sorely tempted—however, I am on a strict high-protein diet.

I am by no means a baseball aficionado—however, I am not totally ignorant of the game. I have, through occasional video viewing, natural curiosity, and longevity, acquired at least a working knowledge of the game and even recognition of certain of the more important individuals in the sport.

From the scoreboard in left field, I learned that I had entered the stadium in the last half of the sixth inning. The home team led the Yankees, 4 to 2, and was at bat. There were two outs, Gary on first base, and Seiler at bat.

I noticed that I was drawing some attention from those seated about me. Perhaps I should have worn one of my sports jackets rather than the red-lined cape.

Seiler walked on four pitched balls, putting men on first and second. Monson stepped into the batter's box and swung at the first pitch. He sent a fly ball to Winfield, the Yankee left fielder, and that ended the inning.

I now became aware of a middle-aged couple standing in the aisle glowering at me. They remained thus for a few minutes more and then departed. However, they soon returned, this time accompanied by an usher.

He regarded me sternly. "Are you sure you got the right seat, mister? These people think you're in one of theirs and they got the ticket stubs to prove it."

The pair nodded confirmation and held up their stubs. "We had car trouble and just got here," the man said.

I managed to look perplexed. "Isn't this Section Eight?"

Obviously it was not and the usher said, "Nope."

I rose immediately. "My apologies, madam and sir. I seem to have made an error."

I left them and wandered up and down the aisles until I found another vacant seat in Section Five.

The Yankees went down one-two-three in the top half of the seventh.

I now found the same usher who had accosted me before at my side. This time he was accompanied by a policeman.

The usher spoke. "I been watching you, mister. This ain't Section Eight either."

I blinked surprise. "It isn't?"

"No. Let's see your ticket stub. If you paid to get in here, you got a ticket stub."

I searched several of my pockets and then chuckled. "I seem to have lost my stub. It was here just a moment ago." Then I appealed to his reason. "Oh, well, what difference does it really make which seat I take? As long as it was empty."

The policeman took the opposite view. "Mister, no stub, no seat." He took me by the arm and began escorting me to the exit.

I could, of course, have tossed him, the usher, and several dozen of the interested spectators to the winds, but I detest being the center of attention. It brings a blush to my cheeks, which can be quite a strain.

The policeman guided me all the way down the exit ramp and out of the stadium before he released his hold.

"For shame, mister. You look like you got money and still you sneak into the stadium."

When he disappeared, I walked to the ticket windows only to discover that they were all closed. Nevertheless, I reentered the stadium, this time finding a place under the roof of the upper grandstand.

The score was still 4 to 2 and remained that way as the inning ended. The Yankees trotted in for their turn at the plate and our team took the field. I watched our pitcher, a young left hander, wind up and throw the first ball of the eighth inning. A perfect strike.

Then I blinked and nearly lost my grip on the rafter.

I stared at the pitcher as he threw a slider for strike two. So *that* was it.

In the top half of the ninth, Piniella hit a home run for the Yankees with nobody on, but it wasn't enough and they lost the game 4 to 3.

After the game I remained in the area waiting for the players to show, change to mufti, and exit.

When they did, some of them went to private automobiles in the parking lot and others to the team bus.

I followed the bus closely as it made its way out of the lot and onto the freeway. It took the team back downtown and debarked them at the Atkinson Hotel.

I managed to be in the same elevator which took Monson, the pitcher, up to the twelfth floor. When he unlocked the door of his room, I shouldered in before he could close it again. He backed up, startled. "Who are you?"

I proffered my card and he glanced at it without touching. I smiled. "I am here to see that justice is done."

He swallowed. "Justice? What justice?"

"Oh, come now. You know perfectly well that I am referring to the murder of one Albert Marshall on an evening two months ago at the County Stadium."

His face paled.

I was rather proud of my deductions and now I proceeded to expound. "Let me refresh your memory, sir. On that night two months ago, you were pitching. However, you were not at your best. You were shelled from the mound and sent to the showers. Being sent to the showers can be interpreted literally or figuratively, depending upon the manager of a team. And your manager was literal. You descended into the bowels of the stadium to the locker room. You removed your uniform.

"I deduce that you had just finished your shower and were still in the shower room toweling yourself when Albert Marshall entered the adjoining locker room, his mission being to pilfer anything portable. If you had been still showering, Marshall would have heard the water running and fled immediately.

"As you reentered the locker room you saw Marshall at work. You sneaked to your locker, removed a pistol from therein, made your presence known, and shot him."

Monson sank slowly into a chair.

I smiled grimly. "Marshall was sorely wounded, but still had the strength to flee. And then suddenly the full realization of what you had done struck you. Even if the man was a thief caught in the act, why does a six-foot-three-inch two-hundred-pound man in the prime of life find it necessary to use a weapon against a middle-aged five-foot thief? It might possibly even be considered murder. You could get into real trouble if you admitted the shooting. So you decided to say nothing at all."

Monson sighed heavily and shook his head. "No. It wasn't like that. It was an accident. The gun didn't even belong to me. It's Seiler's. He has the locker next to mine and he collects guns. He just bought that one for his collection. I didn't know it was loaded and I never held a pistol before in my life. I was just going to point the gun, but I guess it had a hair trigger or maybe I was just too nervous and it went off.

"I was really stunned when it happened. I just stood there, not knowing what to do or think when he staggered out. I was still in shock when the team came in after the game. And then I learned that he was dead and the police thought he was the victim of a holdup attempt."

Monson looked me full in the eye. "I was going to go to the police and tell them what happened, but then all kinds of other thoughts came to my mind. Like this is my first year in the majors and we're pennant contenders. And all my life I dreamed about pitching in a World Series. So I finally decided I'd say nothing until the end of the season or the World Series, whichever came last. And then I'd go to the police and be ready to go to jail, if that was in the cards. But now that you know what happened, I guess I'd better go to the police right now."

I thought over his words. "You say the team is a pennant contender?"

He nodded. "With any luck at all, we'll make it."

I pondered a bit more, pacing back and forth a few times while he watched. Then I came to a decision. "Well, perhaps it won't do any actual harm if you waited until the end of the season or the World Series."

He brightened. "You really think so?"

"You have my permission."

The next evening, I was waiting in my office when Pierce appeared.

He listened while I related the previous night's events and then became reflective. "You really think he'll go to the police after the World Series?"

"Yes, I believe so. He seemed quite sincere to me. I think we can trust him," I said.

"How old is he?"

"I'd guess about twenty-one or -two."

Pierce mulled a bit more. "Well, if it had been murder, like I thought, that would be one thing. But if it was an accident, I can't see what good it will do for the kid to report to the police. I mean it can't do Albert any good. He's dead. And Monson is still a young man. He could ruin his whole life and career. Maybe he should just keep his mouth shut forever and let sleeping dogs lie."

I smiled. "My sentiments exactly. I will speak to him again."

Pierce now asked the question for which I had been waiting. "How did you manage to pinpoint Monson? After all, there are a lot of other players who could have done it."

I chuckled. "When Monson undressed for the showers, I suspect that he tossed, flung, or otherwise draped his uniform shirt over the edge of his open locker door. The name Monson in lower case *and* upside down, means nothing. However, in upper case—as it appeared on his uniform—and upside down, it becomes NOSNOW.

"As you said, Albert knew absolutely nothing about baseball or he might have recognized Monson. But all he saw was someone standing next to a uniformed shirt which carried the letters NOSNOW. As far as Albert was concerned, that could very well have been the player's name. When he conveyed that information to you, he chose to pronounce it 'No snow,' which is as reasonable as any."

After Pierce left, I locked the office and went off to the County Stadium. This time I wore my sports jacket and bought a ticket.

We beat the Yankees again, 6 to 1.

Cardula and the Locked Rooms

"This is a very delicate matter, Mr. Cardula. What I tell you must be kept in the strictest confidence."

"You may trust me implicitly, sir."

He nodded approval. "I am ready to pay generously for your services, Mr. Cardula. Generously."

Usually my clients plead near-poverty when it comes to negotiating my fees. When they volunteer money freely, I am always suspicious. And curious.

Thompson was a thin man in his middle fifties, well-dressed, with well-manicured nails. Blood type B, I guessed.

"Are you a full-time private detective?" he asked. "Not moonlighting from some other job, are you? I mean your display ad in the telephone book specified night hours only, and that rather intrigued me."

"I do not moonlight in any accepted sense of the word, sir. I am simply a night person."

He hitched his chair closer and got to the point. "My painting has been stolen."

"I presume you have already informed the police?"

"No. They are the very last people I want in on this. But I want my painting back. Have you ever heard of *The Feast?* It is Van Gogh's lesser known sequel to *The Potato Eaters*."

I remembered something else. "*The Feast* was stolen from the Andrews Museum of Art some four or five years ago. And yet you refer to it as *your* painting?"

"I paid good money for it."

"You bought it from the thief?"

"About a week after it disappeared from the museum. He came to me."

"And you knew it was stolen?"

He shifted in his chair. "I guess I did. But if I hadn't bought it, he would have sold it to somebody else. I couldn't let that happen."

"It never occurred to you to call in the police?"

He shrugged that off. "All kinds of things could have gone wrong and he could have disappeared forever with it. No, I decided that the only way to recover the work was to buy it from him."

"But you did not return it to the museum."

"Well, not exactly. I felt that since I'd recovered the painting and paid a goodly sum for it—done a public service, so to speak—I should be entitled to enjoy it privately for a few years. I fully intended to return it to the museum eventually." He studied me. "If you take any of this to the police, I will deny everything. Besides, I don't have the painting anymore."

I smiled faintly. "I have no intention of going to the police. My word is my word. So the thief stole the painting and came to you knowing that you might be interested in buying it for your own personal pleasure?"

"I guess you could put it that way. I didn't *commission* him to steal it, if that's what you suspect."

He sighed heavily. "Well, I had the painting and obviously I couldn't exhibit it openly. Therefore I hung it in a room on the second floor of my house. I kept that room locked at all times and I have the only key. When I wished to enjoy the painting, I would let myself in, and when I left, I locked the door behind me."

"No one else knew you had it?"

"No one. At least I thought no one knew, but now I am not at all certain about that. That's why I'm here. If I thought some ordinary thief had stumbled upon the painting and fled with it into the night, I would simply leave the entire matter there. But I have my *suspicions*."

"Has it occurred to you that the man who sold you the painting may have decided to re-steal it with the idea of selling it again to someone else?"

"That would hardly be possible. A week or two after I bought *The Feast*, he was shot and killed on another job by an art gallery guard."

"But in the short time preceding his death, could he not have told someone else that he'd sold the painting to you?"

"Perhaps. Yet why would this unknown person wait five years?" He shook his head. "But whoever stole the painting knew exactly where to find it in my house. And it was the only painting stolen from my collection. Nothing else was disturbed, though I have other masterpieces on my walls, openly exhibited. Not in locked rooms."

"What about your servants?"

"They've all been with me a long time. If one of them had been so inclined, he could have stolen any one of my paintings long ago. Perhaps even all of them. No, whoever stole *The Feast* wanted that particular painting and no other."

He regarded me for a few moments. "Actually, I think I know who stole the painting. Or at least that it's one of two people I'm suspicious of. Their names are Diana McKenzie and Gordon Duffin."

He smiled grimly. "I have always regarded them as friends. Good friends. They too are serious collectors and I have entertained them frequently as guests. Fairly recently I may have made some slip and given away my secret, even to the painting's location in my house." He coughed slightly. "Unfortunately I occasionally drink too much. Just occasionally. And I must have blurted it out on one of those evenings, though I don't really remember to which one of them or when."

He rose. "I suppose you would like to see the scene of the crime? I touched nothing. My car is downstairs."

"Thank you, but I will provide my own transportation."

Actually I am well -acquainted with the suburb in which Thompson lived—I myself have a large sturdy Victorian in a nearby rural area—and since I always take the direct route, I got to his home before he did. I waited in the shadows until Thompson entered his house and his chauffeur-driven car went on to the garages at the back of the house before I knocked on the door. Thompson let me in, offered me a drink, which I refused, and mixed one for himself. He carried it with him as he led me upstairs to the second floor. We passed down the carpeted corridor, turned a corner into a small passageway, and stopped at a door. Thompson produced a key.

When he unlocked the door and switched on the lights, I entered an opulently furnished room of medium size. Thompson indicated a spot on the wall. "This is where it hung."

I stared about the room. "Are you positive none of the servants knew you had the painting? After all, a locked room in a house is something of a challenge."

"I don't ordinarily use this wing of the house at all so I keep all the rooms locked."

"If someone learned that you had the painting and wanted it, why didn't he first make you an offer?"

"Cardula, you may not understand the mind of the dedicated collector. Such a person would know there was really no point in asking me to part with it."

"When was it stolen?"

"I don't know, since I don't come up here every day, but it could have happened last Sunday between one and five in the afternoon. All the servants had the day off. The only person still on the grounds was the gardener, and he was watching a football game in his quarters over the garage. I myself was out on the lake in my boat and didn't get back until five. When I went upstairs to look at the painting, it was gone."

"The thief had used a key to the room?"

"No, apparently he came up the balcony outside. He broke a pane in one of the French windows and unlocked it from the inside." He pulled back the drapes so I could see the broken pane and the glass shards on the rug. "I don't think you'll find any fingerprints. Neither Diana nor Gordon would be that stupid."

I turned about to study the furniture, the rug, the fireplace, even the high ceiling. I was looking for something. But what? Something was missing from this room. Something besides *The Feast*. But I could not for the world of me think what it might be.

Thompson watched me. "I'll get you Diana's and Gordon's addresses," he said. "They both live within a mile of here."

I decided to drop in on Diana McKenzie first, since her place was the nearest. I arrived there at one-thirty A.M. and circled the dark house. On the ground floor I found an unlocked window.

If Diana McKenzie had stolen the painting, where would she keep it now? In some closet for the time being? I moved silently through the rooms, trying various doors. Moonlight streamed in the windows and since I have excellent night vision, I didn't find it necessary to turn on any lights.

I found nothing of any particular interest to me, and yet I frowned. There was something missing here, too. Not the same thing that was missing from Thompson's locked room, whatever that was, but something entirely different. I could think of no answer to either puzzle, however.

On the second floor were guest rooms, all of them unoccupied. When I reached the next-to-last door in the corridor, I found another bedroom but one which had the look and general feel of being used. I opened the door to a closet filled with women's clothes and searched it. Nothing. The next door revealed a bathroom. I tried the third door on the opposite side of the room. It was locked.

Ah, what did we have here? Another closet? Would a bedroom have two closets? And if it did, why would one of them be locked and not the other? Or did the door lead to another room? I got out my set of picks and was about to find out when the lights snapped on.

I turned to see a strikingly handsome woman standing at the light switch. She regarded me coldly. "Are you looking for something?"

It was certainly a most embarrassing situation. I would have blushed had I been able.

I pulled myself together. "Madam, have you ever seen me before?"

"No."

I smiled. "Good." I opened one of the windows at my elbow and leaped to the ground below. As I hastened across the lawn, I looked back. She was at the window watching my progress.

I found Gordon Duffin's house dark and well-secured. I had to use my lock picks to get in.

Once again, on the second story, I encountered empty guest rooms until I opened the fifth door in the hall. A bedroom too, but this one contained a middle-aged man asleep in bed. I tiptoed into the room and opened a door which revealed a closet of clothes and shoes. I opened the door beside it. A bathroom. I tried a third door. It was locked.

I was mildly surprised and definitely curious. I brought out my lock picks again. I stepped through the doorway into what was apparently a room and closed the door behind me. In the absolute darkness I could see nothing. I ran my hand along the wall until I found a light switch and flipped it.

I blinked.

On the wall before me hung a painting. The painting. I stepped closer.

The Feast. A family of peasants in the gloom of a cave-like kitchen solemnly consuming boiled cabbages and staring empty-eyed at nothing.

I looked around me then at this room I had found, and realized instantly what was wanting in Thompson's locked room. It made me think. Considerably.

I would have liked to have taken the painting with me, but it was impossible, aerodynamically. The next evening, therefore, after I rose and dressed, I collected my car from its carriage house. I don't ordinarily use it except in inclement weather when one is in danger of a drenching, or in winter when the cold can freeze the very blood in one's veins.

Thompson answered the door immediately and showed me in. "Well? Have you found out anything yet?"

"Gordon Duffin has the painting."

"You've actually seen it?"

"Yes."

He was pleased. "Wonderful work. And fast." Then he discovered that I wasn't carrying anything. "Well?"

"Well what?"

"Surely when you saw the painting, it must have occurred to you to bring it back?"

"There was a difficulty."

"What difficulty could there possibly be?" Then he chuckled. "Ah, I see what it is. You are retreating behind the technicality that you were being paid to find who took the painting, not to retrieve it? That is another job for which you expect to be paid additionally?" He sighed. "Very well. I've heard about the ethics of private detectives before. I am prepared." He opened a wall safe and extracted a stack of bills. "Thirty thousand dollars. But that's my limit. I won't haggle."

I shrugged. The circumstances of the case were unique, and my home has an open-end mortgage.

There were lights on the third floor of Duffin's house—probably the servants' quarters. Otherwise it was dark.

I let myself in. This time Duffin's bed was unoccupied. I went to work on the locked door.

In my car, I wrapped the painting in a blanket. Tomorrow that Van Gogh was going to be returned to the Andrews Museum of Art.

Thompson would, of course, be furious. He might even demand that I return the thirty thousand dollars, but I would refuse, pointing out that, after all, he had deceived me and I don't think much of deception. Especially when I am the victim of that deception.

I sighed at the perfidy of man. The situation had been the very opposite of what Thompson had presented to me. It had not been Thompson who had bought the painting from the thief. It had been Duffin. It had not been Thompson who kept the painting in a locked room. It had been Duffin. It had not been Thompson who had had a little too much to drink one evening and let it slip out that he had the painting. It had been Duffin.

And thus Thompson needed a leg man. He had concocted his whole story for my consumption, even going so far as fixing up a locked room, staging the theft, and handing me two "suspects."

He had, however, committed one oversight.

Dust.

Or rather the *absence* of dust.

If, as Thompson had claimed, no one but him knew of the painting or had entered the room in five years, then who did the dusting? The vacuuming? I could hardly picture Thompson himself doing it.

But Thompson's room had been nearly spotless, as though it had been gone over within the week, and probably it had.

Duffin's locked room, on the other hand, had dust all over it, and spider webs high in the corners.

I was conscious of an increasing fatigue. When I have not had sustenance for more than a week, I weaken rapidly. I would have to do something about that and soon.

Diana McKenzie answered the knock herself. She stared at me, still unafraid. "Well, well, back again?"

I nodded. "Frankly I just couldn't get you out of my mind. I decided to return and apologize."

I handed her one of my cards.

She glanced at it. "And just what was a private detective doing in my home last night? What were you looking for?"

"A stolen painting. I believe I know what you keep in that locked room."

Her eyes flickered.

"You think I have a stolen painting upstairs?"

"No. Not now. Last night I should have realized you couldn't possibly have stolen the painting. The theft occurred in the afternoon. And when I searched your house, I felt there was something missing from the ground floor rooms—something that should have been there but wasn't."

"And what was that?"

"Mirrors. You have them in your bathrooms and guest rooms, of course, but there are none anywhere else in the house, where you might find yourself in company. I should have guessed it. That magnificent pallor, those eyes, that absolute fearlessness."

Those eyes began to gleam.

"And what is it you keep behind that locked door? Aren't you aware that just a few ounces of your native soil tucked under your pillow is quite sufficient to see you safely through the day? There is no need for the entire box."

"I am a traditionalist," she said stiffly. "I go the whole bit." Her eyes zeroed into mine with an intensity guaranteed to freeze, to mesmerize, anyone on earth, with a few possible exceptions, of which I am one.

She glared for a full thirty seconds and then frowned uncertainly.

I extended my smile past my lateral incisors.

She blinked, and when she could believe, she said, "This is the most incredible coincidence."

I offered my arm.

"I was about to go out for a bite. Would you care to join me?"

She did.

Cardula and the Briefcase

My night hours bring me a great deal of clients who for one reason or another, dare not go to the police for help.

After I assured Alvin Atkins that anything he might tell me was utterly confidential — though I would have refused to cross my heart if he had asked me to do so — he came to the point.

"Mr. Cardula. I am a thief. And so is — or maybe was — Charley Whittle."

I nodded to indicate that I had successfully survived his revelation.

"Charley and me are partners and been that way for about three years. I met him in Waupon and we both got paroled at about the same time."

He hitched his chair closer. "We usually operate at around nine in the evening and mostly apartments. At that time of day. if people aren't home, they're probably making a night of it and shouldn't be back for a couple of hours.

"Well, tonight we were in this apartment building on the east side— one of those posh three-story places. We let ourselves in apartment thirty-one, which is on the top floor, and turned on the lights. It was a real classy place, big rooms, and even a cathedral-type ceiling in the living room—or maybe you'd call it the drawing room. Anyway, I grabbed an electric typewriter from the den and carried it down to the car which we had parked in the lot behind the building. I used the fire stairs and propped open the exit door so that I could get back in that way.

"Going back for more loot, I was a bit surprised not to meet Charley coming down carrying something. And when I got to the apartment door again, I found that it opened only an inch because it was on the chain. So I said, 'Hey, Charley, why is the chain on the door?' But Charley doesn't come to unhook it. Instead he says real fast. "He's got me, Al. He's got a gun and he's going to call the cops. And then there's a thud and a groan.

"I figure what happened was that the owner of the apartment must have been somewhere in there — probably asleep — and he woke up when we let ourselves in and went looking for his gun. it was just my good luck that it happened to be downstairs when he found it.

"Well, there's nothing I can do for Charley, especially if this guys got a gun. because I don't carry one myself. So I don't wait around to hear any more. I race down to the car and speed away fast.

"And I'm not worried about what Charley might tell the cops, because he wouldn't rat on me any more than I'd rat on him.

"The next day — which is today — I buy a newspaper to see what's being said about Charley, but there's not one word.

"Now I wouldn't expect to see anything in the papers just because a typewriter is missing, but if the police picked up Charley in somebody's apartment, that's big enough to mention, isn't it? But nothing."

He paused for a few moments of thought. "Finally I come up with the answer. When Charley gave me the warning, the apartment owner got nasty and slugged him. Probably with the gun.

"But he hit Charley too hard. So there he was with Charley dead and so he changed his mind about calling the cops. They might want to know why he had to hit Charley so hard when he already had him covered with a gun. He could get into a lot of trouble. Bad publicity, if nothing else. Or maybe he's got another reason So he decides that he'll have to get rid of Charley's body himself, and that ought to be the end of it..., His partner would be the last person to go to the police, and he's right.

"I thought about that all day and finally I decided that something had to be done about it. I was going to go to a private detective tomorrow, but when I looked in the phone book for an address I saw that you got night hours. Only. So I came right over."

It was now nearly eleven P.M.

Atkins now wound it up. "Maybe he's still got Charley's body in the apartment. maybe not. The point is that I don't want him to get away with murder if anything can be done about it."

Atkins gave me a phone number where he could be reached, a snapshot of Charley, and the address of the apartment building where Charley had disappeared.

After Atkins left, I went right to work. I decided against using my car. After all it was a balmy night with no threat of rain and a favorable tail wind. Besides, I needed the exercise.

I arrived at my destination in less than ten minutes, using my ring of special keys and picks to enter the security-conscious building. In the foyer, I found that mail box number thirty-one belonged to an H C Jefferson.

At the door of apartment thirty-one, I listened, but did not hear any sounds, TV, or otherwise. I pressed the buzzer several times and waited a full five minutes. No one came to the door.

Was H.C. Jefferson playing possum again? Would he be waiting on the other side of the door with a gun? Would he fire at me point-blank and ruin a perfectly good suit? It was a chance I had to take.

I let myself into the apartment and turned on the lights. First I made a thorough search of the apartment, including the closets, and I even looked under the bed. I found neither H.C. Jefferson nor any trace of Charley. I then searched for blood stains — a pursuit for which I have a talent — but I found none.

The telephone rang.

I let it ring five times and then succumbed to temptation. I picked up the receiver. "Yes?"

"Is this H.C. Jefferson?" a man's voice asked.

I decided to go along with that. "Yes. Who is calling?"

"Never mind. Are you missing anything?"

I gave that a moment's thought. "Maybe a typewriter?"

He chuckled. "Anything else?"

"Maybe."

"How about $200,000 in one-hundred-dollar-bills? When I opened that little briefcase and looked at all that money it all went to my head. It even broke up a beautiful friendship."

I frowned as a suspicion formed in my mind. Was I talking to Charley Whittle? While his partner had been carrying the typewriter to the car, had Charley found the money and decided it was too much to share with his partner? Had he quickly put the chain on the door and then put on his little act, knowing that Atkins would flee from the scene as swiftly as possible? "Why are you calling me now?"

"When I left your place I checked in at a hotel just so I'd have someplace to count the money and I did. About $200,000. I thought I struck it rich."

I picked up the significant word. "Thought?"

"That's right. Then I looked at that money again. More careful this time. And I see they are all new one-hundred-dollar bills. So I get to thinking. Who would leave $200,000 just lying around like that?"

"I don't know what you mean?"

"I was going to take a plane out of town, but then I decided to stick around another day and see what's in the newspapers about $200,000 being stolen. But there's nothing. Not one word. So I come to a conclusion. The bills are counterfeit."

I wisely said nothing.

"If I tried spending them. I'd probably get picked up. Printing counterfeit money isn't my trade. I thought that over all day, and a finally I see some light. And profit. The bills mean nothing to me so I think they mean something to you. If you didn't print them you have to buy them from somebody. And maybe they cost you.

"Possibly."

He chuckled again. "I went back to your apartment building a while ago and got your name off the mailbox. Then I looked it up the phone book and here I am. I could let you have the bills back for thousand dollars. In *real* money."

"Suppose they aren't worth that much to me?"

"Look. I'm really doing you a big favor. I could easily ship the bills to the police with a note telling them where I found the funny money. That might not be enough to pin it on you. but they'd at least be watching you for a while. And that could put a crimp on your operations."

"In other words, you're really blackmailing me?"

"Well, that too. $10,000 is my price. Meet me at the magazine rack in the bus station downtown at twelve noon tomorrow."

"I can't. I have a severe case of heliophobia. Suppose I meet you in about an hour. It'll take me that long to raise the cash."

Charley thought that over and decided it would do.

After he hung up, I sat down to think. My musings were interrupted by the sound of a key being used on the apartment door lock. I quickly adjourned to the shadows of the cathedral ceiling.

A few moments later, a striking young woman entered the room carrying two suitcases. She put them down and sank into a chair with the general relief of someone who has just returned from a long journey and is thankful to be home.

Her hair was raven black, her skin quite arrestingly pale, and she had lustrous black eyes. Exactly my type of woman, and for a moment I even wondered if she might not actually be one of . . . . But no, I could see her image reflected quite clearly in one of the room's mirrors.

I studied the suitcases. Perhaps they explained why the robbery had not been reported to the police. H.C. Jefferson had been away on a trip. Did this mean that the money might be genuine after all?

Suddenly she frowned and sat up, staring past the open door of the den. She rose to her feet and entered the room, coming back out in a matter of moments. She had obviously discovered that her electric typewriter had been stolen.

She went directly into an adjoining bedroom. From my point of vantage, I could see her open the top drawer of a dresser. It was evident that she did not find what she was looking for. Her lips moved in a silent, emphatic oath, and she reached for the bedside phone.

Was she calling the police? I quickly descended and picked up the extension in the drawing room.

I heard the rings and then the phone was was picked up and a man answered.

"Ernie," she said. "This is Helen. I just got home."

"How was the trip?"

"Pretty good. I got rid of about a hundred thousand." She paused. "Ernie, while I was gone somebody got into my apartment and stole my electric typewriter."

He sounded sympathetic. "I read someplace that one out of three households gets ripped off every year."

"The typewriter wasn't the only thing that was missing."

"Oh?"

"I had two hundred thousand in a briefcase. That's gone too."

He sighed. "I told you not to leave that stuff lying around like that Helen. You should keep it in a safety deposit box."

"I know. But it's too late to cry about that now. Whoever stole the bills is going to use them. He's bound to get picked up and he'll probably tell the police where he got them. What do I do now?"

"Just sit tight. If the cops talk to you, play it innocent all the way. You haven't the slightest idea what they're talking about. It's your word against his and yours should be a lot better. I suppose you'll want another batch of bills?"

"Another two hundred thousand. At the same rate?"

"Right. But don't keep them in your apartment anymore." When she hung up, I managed to sneak down the hallway to the door and let myself out of the apartment.

I made my way to the bus depot, but found no trace of Charley in the building itself. However when I traversed the area outside, I located him in a little square across the street. He sat on a bench in the shadows of a large shrub where he had a clear view of the bus terminal and its magazine rack. His right hand clutched a briefcase.

I quickly descended upon him, grasping him by the back of the neck and rendering him instantly unconscious. He would remain in that condition for approximately half an hour.

I checked the briefcase and found the counterfeit bills inside. Beside me, the limp and still unconscious Charley slid off the bench and struck his head upon the sidewalk. I immediately examined him and relieved to find that he was not seriously injured, though a bump was beginning to form on his forehead.

I took the briefcase with me when I entered the bus station and went to a public phone. I dialed Atkin's number.

When he answered, I said, "I found Charley."

"That was quick work. Alive or dead?"

"Alive."

"What has he got to say about all of this?"

"I haven't spoken to him yet. I thought you might want to do that yourself."

"You bet. Where do I find him?"

"In the small square across the street from the downtown bus depot You'll find him lying behind the bench closest to the statue of Solomon Juneau."

I went back to the square and thought through the situation What would Atkins have to say to Charley? Better yet, what would Charley have to say to Atkins? I decided not to interfere with the reunion. When I saw Atkins enter the square, I faded back into the bushes where I could still see and hear.

Charley regained consciousness just as Atkins found him. He sat up and blinked. His eyes quickly searched the ground about him, but of course, the briefcase was gone.

Atkins stared down at him. "Well?"

Charley touched his head, discovered the bump, and groaned.

Atkins tried again. "What happened?"

Charley licked his lips. "It's all coming back to me. Al. Slowly. I'm beginning to remember."

"Remember what?"

"There was this guy. In the apartment. This real big guy and he suddenly popped out of nowhere and pointed a gun at me. And all I could think of is warning you, my partner, which I did. And then he swings this big gun and hits me right on the head and everything goes black."

"How come the cops haven't got you?"

"Well, I wasn't unconscious for long, Al. Just a few seconds. And so when I came to, I maraged to get up and escape."

"Why didn't you show up at the hotel?"

"That's just it, Al. I don't know who I am or where I am. I got amnesia. The worst kind. I don't remember nothing at all."

"Why didn't you look at your driver's license?"

"I did that, Al. But the name didn't help any and the address was Green Bay, where I now remember I got my driver's license. I was just about to catch a bus to Green Bay to see familiar things and get my memory back."

"Then what are you doing sitting here on the grass?"

Charley wrestled with that for a moment. "I suddenly got faint and passed out. I guess that's a reaction to amnesia, Al. But now I'm conscious and got my memory back."

Atkins frowned thoughtfully. "Why didn't any of this get into the papers. Charley? I mean about somebody catching you, red-handed in his apartment and trying to hold you for the police?"

"Al, like I said, he was a real big guy. Two hundred and fifty pounds, at least. And I guess he was ashamed that he let somebody as little as me get away from him and decided it was better just to forget the whole thing and not get any ribbing from his friends."

Atkins looked at the sky and then finally sighed. "All right. Charley, let's see if we can find ourselves a drink."

When they were gone, I went back to the public phone. I looked up H. C. Jefferson's telephone number and dialed.

When she answered, I said, "My name is Cardula. I'm a private detective. I have a client who says that he has something you lost last night. A briefcase. He's willing to return it to you. For a consideration, of course."

"Do you know what's in the briefcase?"

"He hasn't told me."

"Why does he need you at all?"

"He isn't certain what kind of a reception he might get. Therefore he has hired me as his intermediary. I'll be over in about ten minutes."

Actually, contrary to popular belief, I have a high sense of moral rectitude. I do not countenance counterfeiting or the passing of counterfeit bills.

However I thought that by meeting Helen C. Jefferson personally, and fairly often, I might be able to lead her from her path of crime.

It was certainly worth a try.

The Locked Rooms

Upside-Down World

"Are you with me, Regan?"

"Yes," I said.

Albright shook his head. "What would you do if you didn't have to work for a living? Stare at the sky all day and think?"

"I'm listening."

"I know you're listening but try to show it. When you look out of the window, I keep feeling jealous of what it is out there that's got your interest. You're paying ten percent attention to me and my little earthly difficulties and the other ninety percent seems to be bumping around the universe."

"You were talking about Robert Cramer?"

Sam Albright sighed and handed me the folder. "Robert Cramer took out the policy five years ago. His heart was perfect then. Or, at least, sound."

My eyes went over the top sheet.

"But he died of a heart attack?"

"Yes."

"How much is the death benefit?"

"Two hundred thousand dollars."

"There was an autopsy?"

"Of course. One of our company doctors was present when it was performed. Cause of death was a diseased heart. The condition had been developing for two or three years, he estimates."

"But still you want me to investigate?"

"Two hundred thousand dollars is a lot of money. The company *has* to investigate." He rubbed the back of his neck. "As far as I can see, there's nothing wrong, except for one little thing that bothers me. At the autopsy our doctor noticed that Cramer's right hand—the fingers, thumb, and ball of the thumb—appeared to be seared. Not a great deal, but enough so that blisters would have developed if he had lived."

"He burned himself just before he died?"

Albright nodded. "Almost immediately before. Our doctor also extracted tiny fragments of glass from Cramer's fingers and hand. We had them identified at a laboratory. They were pieces of an electric light bulb."

"You're positive he died of a heart attack? He wasn't electrocuted?"

"Definitely a heart attack. An electric shock could have brought it on, but there's no way of proving that. He might have been removing a hot bulb from a socket when it burst."

"Might have been?"

Albright smiled. "The interesting point is that it wasn't mentioned in the account of his death."

"When did he die?"

"Three days ago. He was at the apartment of a friend. A Peter Norton. According to Norton, Cramer dropped in one evening three days ago for a couple of drinks. He seemed to have been loaded before he got there."

"He drank heavily with his heart condition?"

"Either he didn't know about it or he didn't care. Around ten o'clock he became pale and complained that he didn't feel very well. Norton went to get him a glass of water. While he was in the kitchen, he heard Cramer cry out. When Norton hurried back to the living room, Cramer was on the floor and apparently dead. Norton called a rescue squad and they worked on Cramer for about an hour, but it was no use."

"Norton didn't have anything to say about the burnt fingers and the glass fragments?"

"He didn't mention them at all. I'll leave it up to you to ask."

"Who is Cramer's beneficiary?"

"A Miss Helen Morland."

"Miss?"

Albright smiled faintly. "It's even more interesting than that. He had a wife. Thelma. Until six months ago, *she* was his beneficiary."

"Does she know he made that change?"

"I don't know. But she'll find out soon enough."

"Were Cramer and his wife separated?"

"Not that we know of."

"What is the relationship between beneficiary and deceased?"

"We don't know that, either. Technically it's none of our business. We can only guess."

"Can you tell me any more about Cramer?"

"He inherited money, but from what I've heard, he had spent just about all of it. I think he had to scrape to make his insurance premiums."

"Anything on Norton?"

"He's single and he has money. That's about all I know."

I decided to see Peter Norton first.

He had an apartment on the third floor of the Merridith Building on the lake shore.

When he opened the door, I gave him my name, showed him my credentials, and stated my business.

Peter Norton was a big man with small, wary eyes. He frowned. "What is there to investigate?"

"Just routine," I said. "We have to fill out forms."

He let me come in.

I saw only the large living room, but I had the impression that there were at least three or four other rooms in the apartment.

"What do you want to know?" Norton asked.

"Just tell me what happened here the night he died."

He lit a cigarette. "There isn't much to tell. Cramer came here at about eight that night. Wanted a couple of drinks and a lot of talk. Jim Barrows—that's my lawyer—was here and we all had a drink. Then Jim left, but Cramer stayed on. We talked and did some more drinking and then around ten Cramer suddenly got pale and asked for some water. I went to get it. While I was in the kitchen, I heard him cry out. When I got back here, he was on the floor. I called the rescue squad, but that didn't do any good. He was dead." Norton puffed the cigarette. "That's all there was to it."

"What was Cramer doing when he died?"

He frowned. "Doing? Nothing. Just sitting on the davenport."

"At the autopsy it was found that the fingers of Cramer's right hand had been seared slightly and also that fragments of glass were imbedded in them. Would you know how that happened?"

Norton went to the liquor cabinet. "I'm afraid I can't help you."

"It didn't happen here?"

"No."

"Then when he came here, his hand was already injured?"

"I didn't notice. I suppose so."

"Was his hand bleeding?"

Norton flushed irritably. "I told you I didn't notice. Why all the questions about his hand? What's that got to do with his death? He died of a heart attack."

"Yes," I said. I was conscious of the faint odor of paint and turpentine coming from somewhere in the apartment. "Didn't Cramer complain about his hand?"

"He didn't say anything to me." Norton poured a drink and then remembered me. "Care for anything?"

"No, thank you."

"Cramer was pretty loaded when he came here. He was feeling no pain, and you could take that literally. I don't know where he cut his hand."

"How long have you known Cramer?"

Norton shrugged. "Two, three years. Got introduced at some party or other. I don't remember."

"Do you know a Miss Helen Morland?"

He looked at me and then after a while he said, "Why?"

"She's his beneficiary."

Norton's eyes narrowed and a thin, hard smile came to his face. But he said nothing.

"Cramer had a wife," I said.

Norton's hand gripped the glass tightly. "You've never seen Helen Morland?"

"No. I don't know her."

His mouth twisted. "Nobody does. You get the feeling that she's on earth just to look around and decide if there's anything worth being interested in. I don't think she's found anything and I don't think she ever will. If she has any emotions, she's never used them."

Norton swallowed half the drink. "She's not bored. It's not that simple. She's just mildly surprised that anybody else exists and she wishes they would go away. I wonder sometimes if she isn't lonely. If she can get lonely. You almost feel like asking her, 'Where did you come from?'"

"Was Cramer in love with her?"

"Yes," Norton said savagely. "'Everybody who . . .'" He finished the drink. "I'm sorry I can't help you any more about Cramer, Mr. Regan."

I looked out of the window at the frame-to-frame blue of the lake and the sky. "You mentioned that, when Cramer came here, a Mr. Barrows, your lawyer, was here too. Had Cramer ever met him before?"

"No."

"And so naturally you introduced them to each other?"

"Of course."

"And they shook hands?"

"Natura . . ." He stopped.

I smiled faintly. "If Cramer had injured his hand before he got here, I wonder if he would shake hands with anybody. Even if he did, I'm sure that Mr. Barrows would have noticed the condition of the hand and at least made some remark about it. I'll ask Mr. Barrows."

There was silence and Norton glared at me.

"There is one other thing I'd like to mention," I said. "Norton received his injury shortly before, or at the time, he died."

Norton took a deep breath. "All right. Around ten o'clock one of the light bulbs in a lamp burned out. Cramer decided to replace it. He burned his hand when he touched it and it burst. Maybe he just grabbed it too hard. I told you he had a lot to drink."

"The bulb burst and then he died?"

Norton went back to the liquor cabinet. "I didn't even know that he had heart trouble. He just collapsed and died."

"Why did you think it so important to deny that Cramer got cut and burned here?"

Norton waved a hand. "I just didn't think; it mattered. The only important thing is that Cramer is dead."

"Which lamp burned out?"

Norton almost shrugged. "That one over there."

I went to the lamp on the end table next to the davenport. I removed the shade and looked at the bulb.

"What did you expect?" Norton snapped. "I put another bulb in the lamp."

I ran my finger over the bulb and showed it to him. "Dust. A couple weeks' worth."

Norton's face darkened. "I took a bulb from another lamp and it happened to be dusty."

But his fingerprints would have shown in the dust on the bulb—and there had been none. I decided not to mention that for now. I picked up my hat. "Thank you for your trouble, Mr. Norton."

The superintendent-janitor of the building was a thin man with the harassed look common in his job. He relaxed when I identified myself and he found out that I wasn't going to ask him to do something.

"Did you know Mr. Cramer? The man who died here three days ago?"

"I saw him off and on. He always seemed pretty well loaded."

"What kind of a tenant is Mr. Norton?"

The janitor grinned slowly. "Okay. But you have to watch him."

"Why?"

"Like don't shake hands with him until you're sure he doesn't have one of those buzzers in his palm." His grin broadened. "I don't mind too much, though. He's generous to me at Christmastime."

He nodded his head at a thought. "He's got a real sense of humor. Once he had me switch the water faucets in the bathroom of a couple in the next apartment. You know, make the cold water come out of the hot tap and the other way around."

"Did he know the people?"

"Just to talk to, I guess."

"You let yourself into their apartment when they were gone?"

He nodded cautiously. "It was just a joke. No harm done. When they complained to me about their plumbing, I went up there and fixed things right again. But they're still wondering what happened. Mr. Norton and me never let them in on the gag."

"Is Mr. Norton's apartment now in the process of redecoration?"

"Not by the owners of the building."

"But he is having something done?"

"Sure. Been three or four workmen going up there. But I guess they're through. Haven't seen them today."

"When a tenant wants to redecorate his apartment himself, he has to have permission from the owners of the building?"

"That's right. We don't want them to do anything wild."

"And Norton asked for permission?"

"Well . . . he forgot. I talked to him about it, though, and he said he was just having a little work done to make the place more cheerful. So I told him okay. He's a good tenant and he's been here for years."

"Did you see what kind of work was being done?"

"No. I got my own work to do."

When I left him, I drove to Lincoln Avenue. The Cramer apartment was cluttered with oversized furniture. I had the impression it had originally furnished a larger apartment.

Thelma Cramer was dark-haired and tense. "Yes, Mr. Regan?"

I decided to tell her about the change of beneficiary, if she didn't know already. "Mrs. Cramer, do you know that you are no longer the beneficiary of your husband's insurance policy?"

The color drained slowly from her face. "But that's . . . that's impossible. When Bob took out the policy, I *know* that I was designated as beneficiary."

"I'm sorry, Mrs. Cramer, but he changed that. Six months ago."

Her eyes narrowed. "Who is the beneficiary now?"

"A Miss Helen Morland."

"Why didn't your company tell me about this before?"

"It's not our business, Mrs. Cramer. A man may change his beneficiary at any time he wishes and it is up to him to inform the interested parties—if he chooses to do so."

Mrs. Cramer twisted a handkerchief. "She's not going to get away with this. I'll take it to court."

"That's your prerogative, Mrs. Cramer. Do you know Miss Morland?"

She laughed harshly. "I've *seen* her. That much I can say. But whether she really saw me or not, I couldn't say. I was just an interruption, an unimportant interruption."

She was silent for a moment and then continued. "There have been other women in Bob's life. He was that kind of a man. But they were just incidents to him. It was different when he met Helen. I could tell that right away. When I found out who was . . . doing that . . . to my husband, I went to her and asked her to leave him alone. I don't know what I expected. Perhaps a scene. But she looked at me . . . those strange gray eyes studied me curiously for a few seconds, and then she said that as far as she was concerned, I could keep Bob home."

Thelma flushed at the recollection. "He was completely infatuated with her, but she didn't want him. I don't think she wants anybody. After she told me to take back my husband, she just turned and went back to the picture she was painting. I wasn't even in the room anymore. She forgot that I was still there. There was nothing for me to do but leave."

"But your husband kept seeing her?"

"Yes. There was nothing I could do about it." Her face showed perplexity. "I don't think anything ever really . . . happened between them. He even talked to me about her. He told me that he would go to her studio and just watch her. He never knew if she was aware of him or not."

Thelma shook her head. "There's no expression on her face, really. I don't believe she's ever happy or sad, like other people."

"Miss Morland is an artist?"

"I suppose. She paints, but I don't believe she ever exhibits or sells anything. I don't even think she's interested in painting. It's just something to do . . . while she's waiting."

"Waiting?"

Her eyes widened. "I don't know why I said that. But it's true. I feel that she's waiting for . . . something."

"Did you know that your husband had heart trouble?"

"No. He never mentioned anything about it to me."

"Do you think that he knew about it himself?"

"I couldn't say. The last six months—ever since he'd met her—he'd been ill. You could see that. It might have been his heart, but I don't think it was that alone. He drank a lot, although he shouldn't have. He always passed out after a while. He couldn't sleep, and he wouldn't eat."

"How did your husband happen to meet Miss Morland?"

"Peter Norton introduced him." Her hands clenched. "I think he did it just to see how she would affect Bob. Almost a practical joke."

"Who was his doctor?"

"Dr. Farrell. He has an office in the Brumner Building."

I rose. "Thank you for your time, Mrs. Cramer."

I drove to the Brumner Building and took the elevator up to Dr.

Farrell's office. When the receptionist showed me in, I presented my credentials.

"Dr. Farrell," I said. "A Robert Cramer, one of your patients and insured by our company, died three days ago."

Dr. Farrell was a graying man in his middle fifties. He nodded. "I read about that." He had his nurse bring a card from the filing cabinet and studied it. "Cramer's been a patient of mine for over ten years. About two and a half years ago, I noticed the heart condition. I told him about it, trying not to alarm him unduly. I put him on a sensible schedule and gave him all the usual cautions and advice." He looked up. "When I saw him six months ago, the heart condition had considerably worsened. Also, he was in other ways not in the best of health—general rundown condition. This time I impressed upon him strongly the need to take care of himself. Apparently he did not follow my advice."

"His wife said that he didn't tell her about his heart."

"I suppose he thought she'd worry."

"Yes. I suppose that was it."

And then I drove to 231 Brainard Street. It was a four-story building among other red brick buildings, in an older part of the city where quietness remained.

I sat in my car and smoked a cigarette and, when I had finished, I went into the building and up to the studio on the top floor.

Yes, Helen Morland had gray eyes and she watched me without expression while I told her why I was there.

"Did you know that Cramer had trouble with his heart?"

Her lips had been about to say, "No," but then she seemed almost to frown for a moment. She stared at me and said, "Yes. He told me." Then she turned and moved away from me.

"Did you know that you are the beneficiary of Cramer's insurance policy?"

She stopped in front of an easel. "Yes."

"It wasn't my business, but I said, "Why?"

She picked up a brush and painted a single line. "He said he loved me. He had no money, but he wanted to give me something eventually."

"He was giving you his life. Did that interest you?"

She made another line and went over it.

I moved about the room. There were paintings completed and uncompleted and I felt that all of them had been forgotten the moment they had been taken off the easel. Some were representations, some impressions, and often there were just simple strokes, up and down, that meant nothing except to say that she had been thinking of something else when they were made.

"Do you think you have a right to the money?"

"He wanted to give it to me." Her eyes were on me now. "Are you angry about that?"

She had soft light hair, but it was difficult to tell the exact shade. It seemed to shimmer in the sunlight.

"Mrs. Cramer is going to fight the bequest."

"Of course," Helen said. "I expect that. But I don't believe we will get to court. We will agree upon something. I will be satisfied with fifty thousand."

"When Cramer died, his right hand was slightly burned and he had bits of glass in it. Do you know anything about that?"

"No."

I went to the big windows overlooking the rooftops. "What is money to you—fifty thousand dollars of it?"

"It frees time."

"To think of people? Of things? Of ideas?"

"To wonder."

I could see the public library, the castle of books. When I was a boy, I had tried to read them all. Perhaps I should never have tried. And above the buildings, the sky. The top of a cage? I found myself saying, "Do you listen when you look up there? Do you hear anything?"

She was beside me. "So faintly. A music I cannot quite understand." Her eyes were on my face. "Why did you ask that?"

"I don't know." I came back to this time and this earth. "Thank you for your time, Miss Morland. I'll be leaving now."

At the door we looked at each other again and then I turned and went away.

Once during that night I got out of bed and stood at the window. The stars were clear and just a step beyond the reach of the mind.

Someone else was watching them too. Yes.

What was she thinking?

In the morning I saw Albright. I told him how Norton had explained about the light bulb, and I told him about the undisturbed dust on the one I'd examined.

He frowned. "It doesn't sound important, but why would he lie about something like that? Do you think it's worth working on this a little more?"

"Yes."

"You'll talk to Norton again?"

"Yes. But first I'd like to see his apartment when he's not home."

Albright looked unhappy.

"You can get me a ring of keys?"

"Sure, but you just can't . . ."

"I lost the key to my apartment, Sam. I just don't want to bother the janitor."

He sighed. "All right. But if you get caught, the company knows nothing about it." He studied me. "I have the vague feeling that you're actually interested in this case."

"Yes," I said.

Albright left the office for five minutes and came back with the ring of keys. "I haven't used these for fifteen years. I hope locks haven't changed since then."

I phoned Norton before I left Albright's office. There was no answer. I tried again from a drugstore a block from Norton's apartment building with the same result.

When I got up to the third floor, I spent ten minutes at the door buzzer and when that got me nothing, I took it for granted that Norton wasn't home.

I used the ring of keys and on the fourth try the door opened for me. Norton was home.

He sat in an armchair facing the door and his eyes stared at me.

But he didn't move and he never would.

I closed the door behind me and moved closer to him.

Whatever had killed him, it was something that left no mess. There was no gunshot wound, no stab.

I went past him and through the apartment. It was large and well furnished, but whatever Norton's personality, it was not reflected in his furniture. The place was as impersonal as a stage set.

I came to the bedroom, where the smell of new paint lingered. It had the neutral look of a hotel room—twin beds, tables and lamps, and two dressers. I tried the drawers and found that they were empty. The closet was bare.

The room was new. Everything about it was new. I examined the woodwork, the doors, the window framing, the floor moulding. All of them were of wood painted for the first time.

Everything was in order—an average guest room. Everything just the way it was supposed to be except. . .

The switch plate controlling the overhead light fixture was too high. They are usually from four to four and a half feet from the floor. But this one was at face level.

I tried the switch and the overhead light flashed on. I flipped the toggle several more times. There was something else wrong . . . something I could feel . . . yes, I could *feel* it.

I looked at the switch. Normally you press the toggle up to turn on the light and down to shut it off. But this one was reversed—down to turn on the light and up to turn it off.

I went back to the living room and now the wastebasket next to the French desk caught my eye. I extracted brown wrapping paper and string. Beneath them lay scraps of picture molding and torn scraps of heavy cardboard.

I put the pieces together. It had been a framed print, twelve by sixteen inches, and the small lettering at the bottom gave it a name. *The Surrender of Cornwallis.* A column of men, resplendent in their red uniforms were marching from their redoubts.

I smoothed the wrapping paper. The package had come from the Barclay Art Shop on Wells. There were no stamps and so evidently the package had been delivered—probably since the last time I saw Norton alive, or I would have noticed the wrapping in the wastebasket when I had been here before.

Norton had received the package, opened it, and then smashed the frame and tore the print into small pieces.

I studied the pieces I'd put together again. Yorktown, October 1781, and the troops marching out to surrender behind a band that played a tune called . . .

I stared at Norton. He had been a man with money and a man who thought switching water faucets an example of wit. Perhaps . . .

I went through his wallet. Nothing interested me except a small business card.

> Arthur Franklin
> General Contractor
> 2714 Virginia Street
> Boardman 7-8136

Norton's topcoat lay over the back of the davenport. I went through the pockets and in one of them I found a handkerchief stained with faint brown. Blood?

I put it in my pocket and then I went through the apartment again, wiping fingerprints off anything I might have touched.

When I left, I allowed the door to the hall to remain slightly ajar. I wanted somebody to find Norton soon and I wanted to know how he had died.

I took the handkerchief to the Lytton & Brandt Laboratories and after a while one of their technicians came back to me with the report.

"It's paint," he said. "Brown. Or rather auburn. Low saturation, low brilliance. Ordinary, somewhat cheap grade interior gloss paint. Could be used for any number of purposes."

Arthur Franklin's office was a small building in one corner of a yard in the valley under the viaduct on Twenty-seventh. He was a big man who enjoyed the stub of a cigar. "What can I do for you?"

I showed him my credentials. "I understand that you recently did some work for a Mr. Norton?"

He grinned faintly. "Some."

"Just what did you do?"

He thought it over for a moment. "You a friend of his?"

"No. This is my work."

He decided to tell me. "Craziest order I ever had. But it was his money and he wanted it done. Wanted it kept quiet, too. He gave me and each of the boys something extra while we were working so that we wouldn't let anything slip to anybody around there."

Franklin settled back in the chair. "We went through a lot of trouble. Had to change everything. Everything. Put the rug on the ceiling and bolted all the other furniture up there too. We had the chandelier sticking up from the floor."

Yes, I had been right.

"An upside-down room," he said. "Yes, sir. Lot of work for a practical joke, but I guess he could afford it. We put the floor molding on the wall at the ceiling and reversed and hiked up the doors. Had to blank out the windows too and make it look like a wall. Wouldn't want the victim to look out of the window and see that the world wasn't upside down, too."

He savored the situation. "Norton didn't tell me what the room was for, but I could guess. Heard about things like that before. He has somebody up at his apartment and gets him to drink enough to pass out. Then Norton carries him into the room and leaves him there. And Norton waits outside, looking through a peephole."

Franklin chuckled. "His friend comes to, but he's still groggy. He looks around and he thinks he's on the ceiling. The guy gets panicky. He tries to crawl up the walls to get down to what he thinks is the floor. I hear it's a riot."

Yes, I thought, Cramer woke up in the room. The furniture loomed up above him and he was on the ceiling. He would be frightened—terrified. What horrible thing had happened? In a moment he would fall.

Instinctively he had clutched for the nearest thing—the chandelier. His heart had pounded madly and in that instant he had suffered his heart attack and his fingers had crushed the bulb.

"I guess it was a short-time joke, though," Franklin said. "Norton called us back two days ago and he had us tear out the whole thing. A rush job, too. We had to put everything back where it was before. Just exactly."

But you forgot one thing, I thought. You forgot to move the light switch back down to where it belonged and forgot to reverse it.

Cramer had died in the upside-down room and then it had been Norton's turn to panic. Cramer couldn't be found there. There would be publicity. Perhaps even criminal charges.

Norton would have preferred to have Cramer's body out of the apartment altogether, but that was almost impossible. He might be seen carrying it. So he had dragged Cramer to the living room and pretended that he died there. There had been no reason for anyone to search Norton's apartment and discover the upside-down room.

Probably Norton hadn't even noticed the injury to Cramer's hand. Even if he had, he had thought that it was unimportant. Cramer had died of a heart attack and that was the big thing. Why should anyone ask about the hand?

The upside-down room. Perfect in every detail and he had even ordered a special print to fasten to the wall—a final touch. It hadn't arrived in time to be there for Cramer's death, but it had come yesterday or early this morning and he had torn it to bits and dropped them into the wastebasket. The print had shown British troops marching to surrender—marching behind a band playing an old English air, "The World Turned Upside Down."

"I wonder if his trick worked," Franklin said, amused by the idea.

Franklin wouldn't know, of course. He hadn't known Cramer, and hundreds of people die in the city of heart attacks. And when Cramer had died, there had been nothing more specific in the newspapers than the mention that he had died "in the apartment of a friend."

When I left Franklin, I drove past Norton's apartment building. A squad car and an ambulance were parked at the curb.

I went downtown to the main office and saw Albright.

He listened to my story and then shook his head. "It's pretty fantastic, but it still won't help us any except to satisfy our curiosity. We still have to pay the claim. Norton could have gotten into a lot of trouble, but since he's dead, there doesn't even seem to be much point in bringing the story to light."

"It all depends on how Norton died. If he had a heart attack, the case is over."

Albright nodded. "I'll get in touch with the coroner and have him phone me when he gets around to looking at Norton. There ought to be an autopsy. I don't imagine a doctor was around when Norton died."

In the evening I was in my apartment when Albright phoned.

"Norton died of poisoning," he told me, without preliminaries.

"Suicide?"

"Doesn't look like it. No note or anything like that. The police are making it their business now. I just talked to Lt. Henricks. He had the apartment searched from top to bottom. Couldn't find any poison."

"Norton might have swallowed all of it."

"Maybe. But he'd have kept it in something. A box or an envelope. Henricks didn't find anything. And it looked as though Norton had just come home when the poison took effect—his topcoat was lying on the davenport. It seems likely that he was poisoned somewhere else."

"Do the police have any place in mind?"

"Henricks didn't tell me, but I doubt it. This thing is only a few hours old. I imagine he'll start seeing everybody Norton knew."

"When did Norton die?"

"The coroner put it at about eleven last night, give or take a little."

When I hung up, I made a drink and smoked a cigarette. I thought of things and I thought of her. Was she waiting? Would I be like the others? Would it be enough for me to watch and wait?

At ten-thirty I crushed out a last cigarette and drove to 231 Brainard. When I got out of the car, I looked up. Stubby columns of lights pushed up at the darkness from the skylight.

When I opened the street door, I smelled paint.

In the dim hall light it was difficult to make out the exact colors, but I thought that the walls had been painted dark green and the wooden banisters, brown. Auburn.

Six feet up the stairs, almost obscured by the shadow of the railing, hung a WET PAINT sign.

I pushed the buzzer at apartment No. 1.

The janitor was in carpet slippers and about him hung the odor of beer. "Well?"

"When did you paint your hall?"

He scowled. "You got me out here just to ask me that?"

"Yes."

And then he saw my face and he knew that I wanted an answer. "Today," he said uneasily.

"Just today?"

"Sure." And then he corrected that. "Well, it was started the day before. The top floor. My son-in-law started around four in the afternoon. He's got a regular job and this was something extra."

I went up the stairs and behind me I heard him lock and bolt the door.

Helen's eyes went over me when she opened the door and let me in. She smiled softly. "I waited for you."

"Peter Norton is dead," I said. "He was poisoned."

She moved to the record player and turned the volume down slightly. "Yes?"

"Did Norton come here often?"

"He came to watch me and to talk. Sometimes I listened."

"Were you listening when he told you about the upside-down room?"

"Yes."

"Norton was here last night, wasn't he?"

"Would you like something to drink?"

"He was here last night," I said. "The halls are dim and he touched the wet paint. He wiped his hand on his handkerchief, but his fingerprints should still be on one of the banisters. They would prove that he was here last night."

She took two crystal goblets from a cabinet. "The police have not been here."

"They don't know about it. Only I do."

She smiled. "Then I needn't worry."

"Helen, I'll have to tell them."

She looked at me. "But why?"

"This is a murder case."

"And I would be the most obvious suspect? There would be an investigation? The police would find out who I am? Where I was?"

"Yes."

"I would not want that."

"Helen," I said. "Did you kill Norton?"

She held one of the glasses to the light for a moment. And then she said, "Yes."

On the record player the music came to an end. There was a click as another record fell into place. The music returned, but the room was cold.

"You didn't have to tell me."

"You asked. I can't lie to you. You know why, don't you? And you will not tell the police."

I said nothing.

She put down the glasses and moved abruptly to a picture leaning against a chair. "I don't even remember painting this. What was I thinking?"

"Did you have anything to do with Cramer's death?"

"Norton told me he was building the room. I knew that Cramer's heart was bad, very bad. And I knew that Cramer's insurance was in my name. I suggested to Norton that Cramer be his first victim. Norton didn't know why, of course." Her eyes searched mine. "Are you shocked? Why?"

"Suppose Cramer hadn't died?"

"I would have thought of something else."

"Is life or death so simple to you?"

She stared at another painting. "I like blue. More than any other color. I've never told anyone that before."

"Why did you kill Norton?"

"He was going to tell the police about me—unless he could have me. It was not an unpleasant way to die. Sleep in one half an hour. Death in fifteen minutes more."

"But what could he have told them? There was nothing anyone could prove. And he would have gotten into trouble himself."

"He wouldn't have mentioned Cramer at all. He would simply have written an anonymous note to the police. He would have told them about the others. He did not know about all of them, but he knew of one before Cramer and he suspected more."

"How many others?"

"Five." She frowned. "Six. It is unimportant. But they are all dead and the police would find something to harm me. I have not always been Helen Morland." She regarded me. "I cannot go to prison. I would die first. I would kill before I would go to prison."

"Perhaps not a prison."

Her eyes widened. "If others think I am insane, I do not mind. But do you?"

"I will have to go to the police. You know that."

"But we are different from the others. Must we obey their rules?"

"Yes."

Her face was pale. "I have never loved anyone before. Must I lose everything that I have now?"

I said nothing. I could not answer her.

"When are you going to the police?"

"I don't know."

"In the morning. That will be time enough. I will not run away.

There is no place to go now. No one to wait for." She smiled faintly. "A kiss? Our only kiss?"

And then I went home. I drank and I waited.

It was cold dawn when I phoned Helen's apartment. There was no answer and I had expected none.

She had not run away, but she was gone.

And the world was lonely again.

Swing High

The body had been taken away and now we watched the firemen hosing down blood on the driveway beside the Medical Arts Building.

"Nobody saw him fall," Sergeant Allen said. "But two people heard him."

"He screamed?"

"No. But it's like dropping a paper bag of water, Lieutenant. Makes a noise and a splash. A Mrs. Corbin and her husband happened to be passing when it happened. She fainted when she saw what made the mess."

Floodlights illuminated the area where the firemen worked. I walked around a loop of hose and looked up the side of the five-story building.

Allen puffed his cigar. "When you fall, there's only one way to go. Straight down. If he didn't come from the roof, it was from one of those three windows—fifth, fourth, or third floors. He couldn't have fallen less than that or he wouldn't have been in the condition he was."

"Who was he?"

"According to his wallet, his name was Thurmond Fraser. That's about all we know now."

A plainclothesman tiptoed through the water and joined us. "He didn't jump from the roof."

I jiggled the car keys in my pocket. "What makes you so sure?"

"There's only one door leading up there and it's locked. Only the superintendent and the janitor have keys."

"Maybe he found a key that would work."

"It doesn't look like it. There's a thick coat of coal dust on the roof. He'd have had to leave footprints if he'd been up there. There weren't any."

I went to one of the floodlights and had it trained up the side of the building.

"When we got here," Allen said, "the third-and fifth-floor windows were open and people were leaning out. The fourth-floor window was closed and dark. Just like it is now."

"Could he have climbed out of another window and worked his way along a ledge before he jumped?"

"There's no ledge. And he couldn't have climbed out on the sill and closed the window behind him before he jumped. It's only three inches wide."

I glanced at my watch. I had been off duty when I'd heard about this on my car radio. "I guess you can handle this without my help, Sergeant. My wife's expecting me. I'll be home if anything develops."

I walked back to my car and drove to my apartment building.

My wife, Mavis, looked up from the fashion magazine when I entered. "You're late."

When I leaned over and kissed her, she turned a page of the magazine. "I had dinner early. Polly left something for you in the oven."

I went into the kitchen and put the roast on the table.

After a while Mavis appeared at the doorway. "We're going to the Dennisons' tonight. They're having a small get-together. No special occasion."

I wondered if Philip Thompson would be there. Probably, if he knew that Mavis was coming.

"When we get there," Mavis said, "try to look as though you were enjoying yourself."

I glanced up at the violet eyes. I doubted if she really cared whether I enjoyed myself or not.

She studied her manicure. "Don't dawdle. I promised we'd be there by nine."

The Dennison apartment was warm with the noise of a dozen people when we arrived. I took a drink from a tray and found a corner to stand in.

Mrs. Dennison made the rounds and spoke to me. "Any interesting murders lately? A real chiller?"

"Nothing in particular."

She moved on to someone else.

I spent the evening watching Mavis and Philip Thompson. They spoke to each other only rarely, and no one would have known what I did about them.

At the office the next morning, Acting Detective Brooks came to me with the information Allen had left before he went off duty. "The floor plans of the third, fourth, and fifth floors are identical. Each one of the three windows we're investigating is the waiting room of a doctor."

He glanced at the folder in his hands. "Third floor. Dr. Abrams. Internal medicine. Three patients and his receptionist were in his waiting room when it happened. Seven-fifteen. They all swear they saw nobody jump, fall, or be pushed out of their window. And none of them ever heard of Thurmond Fraser before."

He continued. "Fourth floor. Dr. Warner. Dentist. But he had no night hours. The place was dark and the doors locked."

"Fraser still might have managed to get in some way."

"We didn't find any keys on his body and none of the doors to Warner's suite had been jimmied."

"Suppose somebody let him in, pushed him out the window, closed it, and locked up the place again?"

"The only prints on the frame and sill of the window belong to Dr. Warner's dental technician. And at seven-fifteen she was eight miles away having dinner at home with her family and some relatives. We checked that out."

"Maybe someone wearing gloves opened the window."

"He would have been bound to smudge some of her prints. But they were clear."

"So that leaves us the fifth floor?"

Brooks nodded. "Dr. Gavin. Eye, ear, nose, and throat. One patient and the doctor's receptionist were in his waiting room at seven-fifteen. Neither one of them saw anything, and they claim they never heard of Fraser before."

"Where was Dr. Gavin?"

"He didn't get to his office until seven-thirty."

"Did Thurmond Fraser have a car? Was it parked somewhere in the neighborhood?"

"In the parking lot behind the building. So evidently he drove, or was driven, there."

"Did anybody see him enter the building? The elevator operator?"

"Nobody saw him. And the elevator's automatic." Brooks pulled the coroner's report from the folder. "The doc takes an educated guess that Fraser fell or was pushed from the fifth floor or the roof."

"Well, we can't question the roof."

Brooks had been ahead of me. "I've got Dr. Gavin's receptionist and the waiting patient outside. His name is Amos Howell and hers is Clara Nevens." He closed the folder. "Want me here when you talk to them?"

"It won't be necessary. Send one of them in when you leave."

Howell was a tall man who sat down gingerly. "I never heard of Thurmond Fraser until one of your men mentioned the name."

I let him light a cigarette and then said, "What time did you enter the doctor's waiting room?"

"About ten to seven. I had a seven-fifteen appointment, but I like to be early."

"The door to the waiting room was unlocked?"

"Yes."

"Was there anyone else in the room?"

"No. It was empty."

"When did the receptionist arrive?"

"About five minutes later."

"Was the doctor in his office?"

"No. I thought so, but he wasn't."

"Why did you think so?"

"His hat was hanging on the clothes tree."

I made a few lines on the scratch pad in front of me. "How do you know it was the doctor's hat?"

"Well, when he came in…about seven-thirty, it was, and after that man fell…he took it with him into his office."

I went back a little. "You say the receptionist arrived about five minutes after you did. What did she do?"

"She went to the doctor's door and tried it. It was locked and she told me that he'd probably be in in a few more minutes."

"And what did you do?"

"I read a magazine and she did some kind of office work. At about seven-twenty we heard the sirens and they seemed to stop right below us. Miss Nevens opened the window and we both looked down. We saw all those people gathered around the body of that man. We were still there when Dr. Gavin came in a few minutes later. He asked us what had happened. Then he took the hat off the rack, unlocked the door to his office, and went inside. He came back ten seconds later and joined us at the window."

"Does Dr. Gavin have a separate entrance to his office from the corridor?"

"Yes, I think he has."

When I was through with Howell, I had Clara Nevens sent in.

She was small and dark-eyed. "I had supper and returned to the office at about five to seven."

"Was there anyone in the waiting room?" .

"Yes. Mr. Howell."

"After you came in, what did you do?"

"I tried the doctor's door. Sometimes, if the doctor's in, he isn't aware that a patient may be waiting. But it was locked. He wasn't in yet."

"How long have you worked for Dr. Gavin?"

"About a month. His previous receptionist quit to get married."

"Just what kind of an employer is Dr. Gavin?"

She hesitated. "All right, I guess." She colored faintly. "Well, sometimes he's a little too friendly. Or he was. But I told him I just wasn't interested. I have a boyfriend."

I moved the ashtray on my desk back and forth a few times. "Does the doctor wear a hat?"

She seemed a little puzzled by the question. "Why, no, I don't believe so. At least I can't remember ever seeing him wear one."

When she left, Brooks came back into my office. "Find out anything interesting?"

"Maybe. What do we know about Thurmond Fraser?"

"He was in the construction business. Doing pretty well, judging from his address. Married three years ago. First time. He was about forty-five."

At noon I went to Lucco's Restaurant, where I took a table on the balcony. I could look down on the main floor without being seen myself.

Twenty minutes later my wife and Philip Thompson took their usual table below me. It was the third time this week they had come here. They ordered cocktails, they touched hands, they smiled. And when they laughed, I wondered if they were laughing about me. When they left at one-fifteen, I paid my tab and drove to the Medical Arts Building directly.

Dr. Gavin was a large man with thick, hairy wrists and uneasy eyes. He led me into his office and closed the door behind me. "What can I do for you, Lieutenant?"

"Did you know Thurmond Fraser?"

"Is he the man who was killed here last night? No, I didn't."

"He wasn't a patient of yours?"

"No."

"What time did you get to your office last night?"

"About seven-thirty."

I glanced about the room. There was no sign of a hat rack or a hat. I indicated the door to my right. "You have a direct entrance to your office from the corridor?"

The doctor seemed to be perspiring. "Yes, but I seldom use it. Usually I come through the waiting room. I like to see if anyone is here. Some patient may have decided to come early, and there's no point in having him sit there if I can take care of him right away."

"Do you usually come in at seven-thirty? I understand Mr. Amos Howell had a seven-fifteen appointment."

He rubbed a hand on the edge of his white jacket. "I usually try to be here at seven. But last night I stopped off for a sandwich and coffee at the cafeteria down the street."

"On your way back here, didn't you hear the sirens? Didn't they make you curious?"

"I heard the sirens, but we have a number of hospitals in the neighborhood and sirens aren't uncommon."

"Didn't you notice the crowd?"

"I came back from the Wells Street side of the building and I didn't see anything in particular. I just went upstairs and when I got here, Miss Nevens and Howell were leaning out of the window."

I considered asking him about the hat, but then I decided to save that ammunition for a time when I knew a little more about the doctor. I rose, said good-bye, and took the elevator down to the first floor. A pharmacy occupied one suite near the entrance and I went inside. It seemed logical to me that ninety percent of the prescriptions written by doctors in the building would be filled here.

I asked to see the manager, and when he came, I showed him my badge. "I'd like you to go back through your prescription book."

He reached for one of several large volumes. "What should I look for?"

"The name Fraser."

I smoked two cigarettes before he paused at a page.

"Here's something. Fraser. Restorinol. Proprietary name. Ear drops. Do you want to know the date?"

"Who wrote the prescription?"

"Dr. Gavin. He's on the fifth floor." His eyes went back to the page. "She had the prescription filled about four months ago."

I took the new cigarette out of my mouth. "She?"

He nodded. "A Mrs. Helen Fraser."

I was about to pass the phone booth in the lobby when I remembered something else. I phoned my wife.

When she answered, I said, "Mavis, some of the boys at headquarters are going up north for hunting this weekend. They asked me to come along."

There was a pause and then she asked, "What time are you leaving?"

"We'll all meet at Lieutenant O'Brien's house about nine."

"When will you be back?"

"Late Sunday night. Are you sure it will be all right if I go? You won't be lonely?" I wondered if she smiled.

"No. I won't be lonely. I'll probably look up some of the girls."

I looked up the Thurmond Fraser address and drove there.

Helen Fraser had green eyes, a small, speculative smile, and evidently the death of her husband had not been a traumatic experience to her. "Sit down, Lieutenant. Can I get you a drink or something?"

"No, thank you. Could you tell me who was your husband's physician?"

"Dr. Bradford. He has offices in the Stanley Building."

"Did your husband ever see a Dr. Gavin?"

Her eyes flickered. "He never mentioned the name. And I've never heard it before."

Like hell, I thought, but I said, "Do you know any reason why your husband should have gone to the Medical Arts Building?"

"None at all."

"Was he ill? Depressed?"

She drew a cigarette from a pack on the cocktail table. "Not as far as I knew."

"Do you know any reason why he might have wanted to take his life?"

"Was it suicide?"

"We don't know yet."

"And if not that?"

"Possibly an accident. We're working on all possibilities."

She studied me and I had the feeling that if I weren't investigating her husband's death, she might sit closer.

"Did your husband carry an insurance policy?"

She smiled carefully. "It was for only fifty thousand. He was worth ten times that."

I stood up. "I may be back again."

The smile remained. "Of course."

At headquarters, Lieutenant O'Brien dropped into my office. "You still set for tonight? Or will this case keep you in town?"

"I can fold it up for a day or two," I said. "I don't think anybody's going to run away."

"Should I pick you up?"

"No. It's a long way across town. I'll take my car to your place and we can leave it in your garage when we take off." But I wondered whether I would really see him tonight. It all depended on what happened. Or what didn't happen.

I spent the rest of the day at my desk putting together the things I suspected about the Fraser death, the things I knew, and the thing I would have to verify. I thought it had probably gone this way:

Dr. Gavin and Fraser's wife had been having an affair. Fraser had learned about it and had gone to Gavin's office before either Miss Nevens or Amos Howell had arrived. He had found Gavin alone and there had been words, threats. They had led to a struggle and Gavin had killed Fraser.

But then Gavin had been faced with a problem. How could he get rid of the body? He couldn't carry it out of his suite into the corridor. He would certainly be seen. And Miss Nevens was due back in a few minutes.

If the murder had occurred in the waiting room, he had dragged

Fraser's body into his office and locked the door. A short while later he had heard Howell enter the waiting room, and a few minutes after, Miss Nevens. He was trapped in his own office with Fraser's body.

Should he quietly leave his office through the corridor and phone back? Should he tell Miss Nevens he wouldn't be in that evening and have her cancel all appointments? Should he come back later, in the early hours of the morning when no one was likely to be about, and somehow get Fraser's body out of the building?

But then possibly he remembered the cleaning women. They had keys to all the offices. Would one of them discover the body before he could return to get rid of it?

Should he simply drop Fraser's body out of the window? But then surely the police would retrace the body's fall to his own office window. He would be questioned. Investigated. Inevitably they would discover the connection between him and Fraser's wife. And then some idea had come to him. There *was* one way to make it appear as though Fraser had fallen from another window.

I smiled wryly. But what *was* that idea? I thought about that for a while and then decided to skip over that blank spot for the time being.

So Gavin had arranged the fall and then had silently left his office by the corridor door. He had remained away until he heard the sirens and then returned and found Howell and Miss Nevens at the window of the waiting room. But he had also seen something else—Fraser's hat still on the hat rack.

There had been only one thing to do. He had taken the hat into his office, pretending it was his own, and hoping that neither Miss Nevens nor Howell would notice—or mention it if they did. Later that evening he had probably gotten rid of Fraser's hat.

I considered some other possibilities. Had Gavin and Mrs. Fraser conspired to murder Fraser? That seemed unlikely. If they had, they would certainly have arranged for Fraser to die in some place other than Gavin's office.

Had he told Mrs. Fraser what had happened? I doubted that too. He would gain nothing if he did. He would simply add to his danger, something he'd try to avoid.

Did she suspect what had happened? Perhaps. But she wouldn't go to the police. The death of her husband apparently meant little to her, and she had the consolation of his estate if it did. If she went to the police, her affair with Gavin would come out into the open. I didn't think she wanted that. I glanced at my watch and then put all the information I had on the case in my desk and locked it.

That evening Mavis watched me pack. "Aren't you going to change to your hunting clothes?"

"I have to drop in at headquarters first to sign a couple of reports. I'll change when I get to O'Brien's place." I picked up the duffel bag and the cased rifle. "Good-bye, honey."

She almost shrugged. "Have a good time."

Downstairs, I put my gear in the trunk of my car and drove a block and a half before I made a U-turn and parked. I waited.

Thirty minutes later Philip Thompson's car pulled up in front of my apartment building. Mavis must have been waiting. She came out of the building carrying a small overnight bag.

I followed them down Humboldt and across the bridge to the East Side. The buildings here were tired and old, and the streets dirty and badly lit. His car turned into a parking lot behind a shabby red brick hotel.

I parked in the shadows half a block down the street and watched my rearview mirror. They reappeared around the corner of the building and entered the hotel.

I lit a cigarette and smoked it, and then another. I took the .38 out of my pocket and checked it. Two cartridges would be enough. Or would I use a third one on myself? I wasn't sure about that much yet.

I walked back to the hotel and entered the lobby. It was musty and empty, and there was no one at the desk. Probably the night clerk had gone out for coffee. I swiveled the register. They had signed as Mr. and Mrs. Charles Swanson. Room 406.

I glanced up at the old-fashioned pendulum clock hanging on the wall. It was almost eight-thirty. I started for the elevator, but then I stopped and turned. I stared at the clock for almost a minute. And then I smiled.

My eyes went to the keyboard. The key to 406 was gone, but 408 was still there. With hotel numbering, that would be the room next door.

I stepped around the desk and was about to reach for the key when I changed my mind. Someone might notice and remember that the key to 408 was missing. But the clerk probably had a set of duplicates somewhere about.

I searched through drawers until I found a jumble of keys. I put the one tagged 408 into my pocket. I went to the switchboard and made the connection to room 406.

When Philip Thompson answered, I slurred my voice. "Hello, Charley? This is Fred."

"Fred?"

"Sure. Remember the Sportsman's Bar? Toledo?"

"Look, mister," Thompson said irritably, "I never heard of you before and I've never been in Toledo. You got the wrong party."

"Now, Charley," I said, "don't give me that. Not to an old pal. I'll be right up with the bottle."

"Hold it!" Thompson snapped. "Where are you?"

"In the lobby."

Thompson swore. "I'll be right down."

I went to the automatic elevator and rode it to the fourth floor.

When the door slid back, Thompson was just approaching. He had been frowning angrily, but now his eyes widened as he saw me and the .38 in my hand. His face whitened. "Wait a minute, Mike—"

"Shut up," I said. "Turn around and keep walking. All the way to room 408. And no talking either."

He walked slowly, glancing back apprehensively. I followed him to 408 and unlocked the door. "Get inside." I closed the door behind us.

"Mike," he said quickly. "I can explain. You can't—"

"Shut up," I said again. "Turn around and face the wall."

He did as he was told. "Mike—"

I reversed my pistol and brought the butt down hard on the back of his head. I caught him as he fell and lowered him to the floor.

I went to the window and used my handkerchief when I opened it. Below me, the sparse evening traffic moved slowly by. I leaned out and looked to my left. The lighted window belonged to room 406—where Mavis waited for Thompson to return.

I turned out my own lights and dragged Thompson to the window. Now I would get rid of him in the same way Dr. Gavin had gotten rid of Fraser.

I draped Thompson over the sill, and bracing my feet against the radiator, I grasped his ankles and eased him all the way out of the window. And then I began swinging him slowly back and forth, back and forth . . . like the pendulum of a clock. And when the arc was big enough so that I thought he would fall to a point almost directly below the window to my left, I let go.

I watched him fall and land and then I closed the window. I locked the door and went down the rear stairs. When I got to my car, I could hear sirens in the distance. I drove on to O'Brien's house.

I ran into Dr. Gavin in a downtown bar almost eight months later. We nodded and I ordered a bourbon and water. He stirred his own drink. "Anything new on Thurmond Fraser?"

"No. The case is pretty much stalled."

"You don't even know if it was an accident? Or suicide?" He hesitated. "Or anything else?"

I smiled slightly. "I don't want to destroy your confidence in the police force, but there are some cases we never do solve."

My drink came and he pushed a bill toward the bartender. "This one's on me."

I sipped the drink. Yes, I could have solved the Fraser case and sent Gavin to prison. But if I did that, someone else might have begun to wonder what really had happened to Philip Thompson.

And so I had altered my reports to eliminate any mention of Fraser's hat and the fact that Gavin and Mrs. Fraser had ever known each other. Anyone reading them would find a case that ran up against a blank wall.

Gavin cleared his throat. "I've been reading about . . . about your wife in the newspapers. Do you really think she pushed Thompson out of that window?"

I tried to sound positive. "Of course not."

"But her fingerprints were on the windowsill."

"She heard the sirens below," I said. "It was natural for her to go to the window, open it, and look down."

"But if she didn't push him out of the window, and if he didn't jump—and she admits that—then just what do you think really *did* happen?"

"I don't know," I said. "But the jury thought it was murder."

He glanced at my reflection in the bar mirror. "I admire the way you stood by her at the trial. I mean—under the circumstances—she was with another man . . ." He stopped and watched the bartender mix a drink. "Twenty years. That's a long time in prison. Especially for a woman. By the time she gets out she'll have lost . . ." He let it hang there. "Do you get to see her sometimes? Visitors' day?"

"Yes," I said. "Once a month."

And I enjoy every minute of it.

Pearls Before Wine

Diana sighed. "I know it's a desperate measure, Henry," my wife said, "but why don't you consider that job with Uncle Wilfred? He's really quite fond of you and it *is* an executive position."

I shook my head. "I will not cadge upon your relatives. I much prefer to collect the insurance on your pearls." I lit a cigar. "I shall invite Detective Inspector Murdock, of course."

"The one who has such trouble with his grammar?"

"But nevertheless a brilliant mind. And that is exactly what we want in this case—a brilliant mind absolutely stymied. We will also invite a half a dozen of our usual dinner guests and Edwin Porson."

Diana frowned thoughtfully. "Edwin Porson? I don't believe I ever heard of him."

"Of course not. I myself have barely a nodding acquaintance with him at the club. However we need his presence. He was one of Mrs. Olliphant's house guests when her safe was looted."

Diana smiled. "Ah, I see what you are up to, Henry. You don't want any of our friends suspected when my pearls disappear."

"Exactly. I prefer the burden of guilt to fall upon a relative stranger."

"Do you suppose anyone will notice that I'm not wearing the genuine pearls?"

'Of course not, my dear. Only an expert can tell the genuine from the imitation and then only after a thorough examination, possibly even X-rays."

I smiled. "To recapitulate. We will be dining and I shall see to it that Jones finds it necessary to go to the cabinet for the red port. When he turns on the small lamp, it will cause a short-circuit and throw the room into total darkness."

Diana nodded. "I will immediately slip off my pearls and hand them to you."

"Right. And as soon as there is sufficient illumination again, you will scream and announce that your pearls are missing."

Thursday evening came and during the beef course, Jones went to the sideboard and pressed the lamp switch. There was a crackle, some sparks, and every light in the room went out.

Diana slipped the pearls into my hand and I raised my voice. "Jones, I believe there are some candles in the sideboard."

Jones struck a match and proceeded to light the candelabra.

My wife clutched her throat and screamed. "My pearls! They've been stolen!"

Inspector Murdock rose and backed against the closed doors. "Don't nobody leave."

He opened one of the doors just slightly, attracted the attention of an outside servant and directed him to phone the police and see to the fuse box in the basement.

Light was restored shortly and the police arrived.

Murdock quickly ascertained a number of essentials and then spoke. "There are only two ways to get those pearls out of this room But those French windows are locked and as far as the doorway is concerned, if anybody had opened one of the doors even a little, we would have all noticed it became while it was pitch dark inside here, the light in the next room was still bright."

Murdock's eyes went about the room. "In other words, them pearls— and the thief—are still in this room."

I was one of the first to be led out of the room and thoroughly searched. Of course, nothing was found.

When I returned to the dining room, Edwin Porson was escorted out for his turn.

I was about to drop the information to Murdock that Porson had been one of Mrs. Olliphant's house guests, when my wife reached for the sugar bowl and her arm brushed against my water glass.

It tipped over.

My first impulse was to reach for a napkin and my second to swear. Both of them would have been futile.

Instead, we watched as the acid instantly ate through the tablecloth and began working on the wood.

Murdock frowned.

My wife managed to laugh lightly. "I just remembered. I wasn't wearing my real pearls tonight. Just the imitations."

It was some fifteen minutes later that Murdock announced that with the help of one of his detectives he had solved everything. "Porson dropped the pearls into the acid and they dissolved."

"Why should he do that?" my wife asked.

"Because he was cornered," Murdock said. "And he had that acid handy for just such an emergency."

"But he denies taking them," Diana said.

Murdock smiled. "It doesn't matter. Like you said, the pearls were imitations and we couldn't put him away for long for something like that anyway. No, it's lucky one of my boys remembered the description of the cuff links."

I was still a bit dazed at the sudden turn of events. "So you maintain that Edwin Porson not only stole the Olliphant jewelry, but he had the gall to wear Mr. Olliphant's cuff links to my home?"

I cleared my throat. "And he also had the presence of mind to push his glass of acid in front of me in an attempt to divert suspicion from himself?"

Murdock nodded.

When he was gone, I turned to Diana. "Why the devil did you have to blurt out that the pearls were just imitations? We could still have collected the insurance."

"I'm sorry," Diana said. "But I thought Murdock really had you when I spilled your acid. I tried to soften the crime, so to speak."

I sighed. "When Murdock's eyes went over all of us a while back, felt just like—well, like a thief."

"I know, dear," she said. She reached for the sugar again without spilling anything this time, "It's really a very fine executive job, Henry. And Uncle Wilfred I wouldn't mind if you took off now and then for a round of golf."

I nodded. "Perhaps everything turned out for the best. I'll see him first thing in—" I stared at her. Had she deliberately over-turned—

Impossible.

But nevertheless I had the feeling that whenever the subject of pearls—or acid—entered our conversation in the future. Diana would look innocent.

Just as now.

Play a Game of Cyanide

Children," Miss Wicker commanded, "tell the detective where you hid the cyanide."

But Ronnie and Gertrude simply smiled up at me and said nothing.

I held one of the sodium cyanide pellets between thumb and forefinger. It was cloudy white in color and approximately one and one-quarter inches in diameter. "They all look like this, children, but they aren't candy. They definitely are not candy and they are not meant to be eaten."

"Ronnie and Gertrude are wretched, evil children," Miss Wicker declared firmly.

Their mother, Mrs. Randall, flushed, but she said nothing.

Originally there had been nine of the pellets. We had recovered four from the grounds outside and another concealed in a toy train in this room. But four of the pellets still remained unaccounted for.

"Are you really a detective?" Ronnie asked. He was seven and younger than his sister.

"Yes. Now, Ronnie, where have you children hidden the poison?"

"Where's your partner?"

"I don't have a partner."

"Why not?"

"I'm a detective-lieutenant. Detective-lieutenants don't have partners."

"Why not?"

I had the impulse to strangle. "Because they're mean and nobody will work with them."

We were in the children's playroom. It was by far the gloomiest and most remote room in the large Victorian house.

I turned to their mother. "Can't you do anything about them?" Mrs. Randall was a pale, frightened woman. "I'm sure they'll tell you in time, Lieutenant. But now they're in one of their stubborn spells and nobody can get them to do anything."

"Bad blood," Miss Wicker said. "Their father was a salesman."

Gertrude was almost nine. The pilot light of mischief danced in her blue eyes. "We live on bread and water."

Miss Wicker glared at her. "I provide you and your mother with a roof over your heads. You ought to be grateful."

"The bread is moldy," Ronnie said. "And sometimes the water has salt in it."

My men were outside searching the grounds again. They had been through the house too, but without success.

I forced a smile. "Come now, children, we've been at this for over two hours."

"What are they good for?" Ronnie asked.

"For cleaning jewelry. Seems odd that cyanide should be used for that, but it's a fact."

"We don't have jewelry," Gertrude said. "But Aunt Agnes has."

Miss Wicker's eyes narrowed. "Have you been prying again?"

I realized now that I had made a tactical error, but I hadn't wanted to alarm the household unless it was absolutely necessary. I had ordered the grounds searched first, and the children had evidently watched from the windows and decided that we were playing a delightful new game.

My smile was beginning to pain me. "That was really very clever of you children to hide a pellet in the toy train. Which one of you did that?" '

"You'll never find out," Ronnie said smugly. "We wiped off the fingerprints."

I sighed. "I think the time has come for a good all-around spanking."

Miss Wicker heartily agreed, but an uncharacteristic firmness came into Mrs. Randall's face. "No," she said. "You will not touch the children."

I rubbed the back of my neck. "We'll have to search them."

Ronnie broke into a grin. "I'm clean."

Why didn't Ronnie's mother give him a haircut, I wondered irritably. He looked as though he were wearing a combed helmet.

"I'll wait until a policewoman comes," Gertrude said demurely.

She was blond and tricky-smiled and would undoubtedly cause a great deal of trouble during the course of her life.

"I will search Ronnie," I said. "And your mother will search you." We found nothing.

"Why don't you search Aunt Agnes?" Ronnie asked.

Miss Wicker bristled. "I do not have the pellets."

"I wouldn't trust nobody if I was a good detective," Ronnie said.

I had the temptation to give the boy a haircut myself. I studied the grin on his face and a thought descended. Little boys simply do not keep their hair combed. Not for two hours at a stretch.

"Ronnie," I said firmly. "Come here!" And when he hesitated, I added, "Right this minute! And bring your head."

I found another one of the pellets.

The little fiend had Scotch-taped it to his skull and combed his hair over it.

I forced myself to beam. "That was very ingenious of you, Ronnie. Now tell Uncle James where the other three pellets are."

"You're not my uncle."

I approached the problem from a tangent. "How would you two like some ice cream?"

A conference of glances united them. They would love it.

"Fine. And I'll see that you get all the ice cream you can eat just as soon as you tell me where the rest of the cyanide is."

They rejected the offer.

"I'll give you a dollar each," I said desperately.

Ronnie was not swayed. "We're holding out for a million dollars."

"I'll make it two dollars each. That's almost a million."

"No, it isn't. I can count up to a hundred and I know."

I found myself pacing the floor. The grounds surrounding the house were extensive. We knew that the pellets had been thrown over the wall near the gatehouse, but the children had been playing in that area when we arrived. Now the poison could be anywhere, and it might take weeks before we found it all.

"Are you positive there were nine pellets?" Miss Wicker asked.

"Absolutely."

Miss Wicker thought and frowned. "Why would anyone want to steal them?"

"The thief didn't know what he was stealing. He just emptied the jeweler's safe and put everything in a bag. Later, when he parked at the curb outside your grounds to examine his loot, he discovered the pellets. In a fit of exasperation, he threw them over your wall."

Mrs. Randall was shocked. "On these grounds? What a horrible man."

"He didn't know what they were. When we caught him, he still had everything from the safe but the pellets. But he did remember where he had thrown them."

Gertrude looked up at me. "Would you read us a story, Uncle James?"

"I am *not* your Uncle James," I snapped. But then I caught myself and smiled. "What would you like me to read?"

The children came to an agreement on *Lennie, the Giraffe with the Short Neck*. Mercifully, it was short.

I closed the book. "And now, children, where are those cyanide pellets?"

Ronnie blinked. "We didn't promise anything."

I had always regarded the Children's Crusade as a great tragedy. I was not quite so certain now. "Children, do you know what a tacit agreement is?"

They didn't.

"A tacit agreement is one in which two parties agree upon something without actually putting it into words or writing it down. Now why do you think I read that revol—that story to you?"

Ronnie grinned. "You thought that we'd tell you where the poison is."

I nodded. "Now would I have read the story if I hadn't expected you to do just that?"

"I guess not."

"But you let me read it anyway, didn't you? You didn't stop me?"

He admitted the fact.

"So, in effect, because you let me read the story we entered into a mutual agreement—a tacit agreement—that you would tell me where the pellets are. Now wouldn't your conscience bother you if you didn't tell me?"

"No."

"Ronnie," his mother said. "I don't think you're being nice. You really ought to tell Uncle James where they are."

Ronnie didn't agree.

"Just one?" Mrs. Randall coaxed. "Just where one itsy-bitsy pellet is. That won't hurt you, now will it?"

The children had a whispered consultation, and then Ronnie came forward. "All right. Just one. I threw it on the roof. Maybe it's in the rain gutter."

I went outside, where Sergeant Davies was supervising the search.

He scratched his head. "We haven't turned up any more."

"Have you ever thought of looking up?"

"Up?"

"Yes," I snapped. "On the roof. In the rain gutters. Check the chimney too."

His head must have itched again. "I never thought of that."

"Of course not," I said irritably. "You're just an adult."

I went back into the house and rubbed my hands. "Well, children, shall I read you another story?"

"No," Ronnie said definitely. "We don't want no more tacit agreements."

"It's time for your nap now," Mrs. Randall said.

I glared at her. "Nobody closes an eye until I find the rest of that cyanide."

But Mrs. Randall was uncompromising. "The children are tired. They will have their nap."

Miss Wicker left the room, but I stayed. I found an adult chair and sat down.

Mrs. Randall opened a sofa bed and the children lay down. She read them a story—*Stanley, the Station Wagon*—and then adjusted the Venetian blinds.

She tiptoed across the room and sat down beside me. "Aren't they sweet?"

Sergeant Davies came into the room. He saw the children drifting off to sleep and lowered his voice to a whisper. "I found another pellet. It was in the rain gutter."

"Well, good for you. Did you search the chimney too?"

"Do I have to?"

"Get back up there."

"I'll get my suit all dirty."

"Davies," I said patiently. "After all, you *are* a sergeant. You outrank everybody out there."

He brightened. "That's right. I'll send Travers down the chimney."

When he was gone, I turned to Mrs. Randall. "Your husband . . . ?"

"He died two years ago." Mrs. Randall sighed. "He left no money and so we came to my aunt's place to live."

I thought about Miss Wicker and the general atmosphere of this place. "There was no place else to go?"

"No. Aunt Agnes is the only relative I have. And then, too, she's alone in the world and I thought . . ." She hesitated. "Well, I thought about going to work first and then I decided against it. I think a mother should be with her children, no matter how difficult things might get."

It was quiet in the room and after a while I nodded myself.

"Pellet."

I sat up. "Did you just hear somebody say 'pellet'?"

"That was Ronnie. We had cottage cheese and chives for lunch. He always talks in his sleep when he has that."

I left my chair and went to the sofa bed. Ronnie's eyes were closed and he breathed gently.

"Don't wake him up," Mrs. Randall whispered.

"That was the last thing I had in mind." I sat down beside Ronnie and waited. He said nothing more.

I prompted him softly. "You were talking about a pellet, Ronnie."

But Ronnie slept. Evidently he hadn't eaten enough cottage cheese and chives to speak further.

"Ronnie," I whispered, "when you wake, you will tell me where the pellets are. Do you understand? When you wake you will tell me where the pellets are. When you   "

"What in heaven's name are you doing now?" Mrs. Randall demanded.

"I'm trying post-hypnotic suggestion." I leaned closer to Ronnie. "When you wake, you will—"

"Stop that!" Mrs. Randall commanded. "I will not have you tampering with Ronnie's little mind!"

I sighed and got off my knees. Perhaps it wouldn't have worked anyway.

After a half an hour the children began stirring.

"Children," I said sternly. "I've had enough of this."

"First let them have their graham crackers and milk," Mrs. Randall said. "Would you like some milk too, Lieutenant?"

I wasn't thinking about milk when I said, "About three fingers."

I waited impatiently while the children indulged in their food orgy.

Those two remaining pellets had to be somewhere. The grounds had been searched. The house had been searched. The children had been searched. I was even willing to search myself if that would do any . .

The thought that struck me was frightening.

Mrs. Randall was alarmed. "Are you ill, Lieutenant?"

Certainly I was perspiring. Those little monsters couldn't have had the gall, the unmitigated nerve, the satanic imagination to—

But they had.

I found another pellet.

It was in the cuff of my trousers.

I recovered from that slowly. At least now only one pellet remained to be found. I thought I might attack the problem by the process of canny elimination.

I smiled. "Children, your little game is over. I know where that last pellet is."

They were dubious.

"Yes, sir," I said, almost bubbling. "It's outside on the grounds."

Ronnie laughed with the delight of superior knowledge. "Oh, no, it isn't. It's in the house."

Gertrude favored him with a fierce frown.

I had outwitted the little imp. "A slip of the tongue," I said quickly. "I really meant to say that I know the pellet is inside the house and it's—" I divided the house into two sections. "It's on this floor."

But they weren't taken in this time. Their silence was infuriating.

Mrs. Randall smiled. "They're such intelligent children."

I glared at her. "Whose side are you on?"

"The law's, of course," she said hastily. "But can't we be sportsmen?"

Anyway, I had established the fact that the last pellet was in the house. I would have to call the search detail back inside and have it go over the building again.

Gertrude seemed to read my mind. "You'll never find it."

I had that feeling too.

"Let's march," Ronnie said.

I looked at Mrs. Randall.

"Sometimes I play the piano," she explained. "And the children march around in a circle. They wear paper hats and blow horns and beat drums. "

I dug into the reservoir of my courage. "I'll join them."

The children regarded me with justified suspicion.

Frankly, I had hoped to lure them into another tacit agreement, but I could see that such a thing wouldn't work this time. On the other hand, I had just committed myself and possibly the children might be antagonized if I backed out now. I created a smile. "This is on the house. I've always wanted to go around in circles."

"We'll have to close the door and put a carpet against the bottom of the door," Gertrude said. "Aunt Agnes doesn't like us to make noise. We plug the keyhole too."

When that was done, Mrs. Randall played the upright piano. The children and I marched. Really a stupid business.

The door opened and Sergeant Davies almost tripped over the carpet. He froze in his tracks when he saw me.

I stopped blowing my horn and put it behind my back. "Well? What the devil do you want?"

He swallowed. "Travers didn't find anything in the chimney."

"Of course not," I snapped. "The last pellet is somewhere inside the house."

"The last pellet? Then you found another one of them? Where was it?"

I flushed. "Never mind that."

"I'll bring the boys in here," Davies said eagerly, "and we'll really tear the place apart this time."

"No," I said. "I'm taking care of this myself." I was not in the best of temper. "Why are you standing there like that and gawking? Get back outside and search!"

"But you just said the pellet's in the house."

"I don't care what I said. Get out!" Another thought touched my mind. "Davies!"

He had been almost out the door, but he stopped.

"Davies, if you breathe one word . . ."

He shook his head almost sorrowfully. "I won't tell a soul what I just seen. They wouldn't believe me anyway."

When he was gone, we readjusted the carpet at the door and resumed marching.

After a while Mrs. Randall stopped playing. "I think that's enough for today, children. The lieutenant is winded."

I sat down gratefully and pondered my next move.

The scream that floated down upon us pierced through our sound-insulated room.

Mrs. Randall's hand went to her mouth. "That's Aunt Agnes. I'm sure she must be in her room. It's the first one at the head of the stairs."

I pulled open the door and dashed up to the second floor.

Miss Wicker lay gasping on the thick rug, her eyes wide with fright and pain and coming death.

I kneeled over her for a moment and then went to the phone. I dialed for an ambulance, but Miss Wicker was dead before I completed the call.

I put down the phone and looked down at her. A teacup lay just beyond the tips of her fingers.

My eyes went to the side table—to the silver tea service, to the thin slices of lemon on a saucer, and to the sugar bowl.

The sugar bowl.

Mrs. Randall and her two children stood in the doorway.

Gertrude looked up at her mother. "Now we won't have to put the rug in front of the door anymore, will we, Mommy?"

We had been looking for a pellet. But it wasn't a pellet anymore.

Someone had crushed it into a powder and . . .

Gertrude?

Or was it Ronnie?

He had a peculiar little smile on his face.

Or Mrs. Randall?

There was something about her eyes. . . .

Or all three of them?

I had the tired feeling that I would never know.

Box in a Box

When Ralph and I reached the scene, the large bedroom was noisy with uniformed policemen, technicians, medics, and photographers fussing around the perimeter of the body.

Ralph put two fingers into his mouth and whistled.

Damn, I thought, *I've never been able to do that.*

A silence of sorts ensued and then a short round man in his early fifties spoke up. "I'm innocent. I've been framed."

I regarded him sternly. "You will have your opportunity to speak later."

"What's wrong with right now?"

I conceded the point. "Very well, who are you?"

"The murderer." He quickly amended that. "I mean everybody thinks that I murdered my wife Hermione but I didn't. My name is Eustis Crawford."

Ralph and I took Eustis Crawford into an adjoining room where we found a tall thin man wearing a hearing aid and a dark haired woman in her thirties waiting.

The tall thin man made the introductions. "I am Oglethorpe Wesson. And this is my sister Genevieve." He regarded Eustis Crawford coldly. "Eustis murdered his wife, who is, or rather was, our aunt. He and Hermione were the only people in their bedroom when she died. The windows and the doors were bolted from the inside. When Genevieve and I finally succeeded in entering, we found Hermione dead on the floor and Eustis unconscious on the floor beside her with a revolver in his hand. Obviously he had fainted after he shot her."

"I did not faint," Eustis Crawford said stiffly. "I definitely did not faint."

Oglethorpe snorted. "You're always fainting, Eustis. Last week, you passed out in the garden when you thought you'd been stung by a bee. And yesterday, when you tweaked your finger in the liquor-cabinet door. You faint whenever you're under any kind of stress and I submit that murder is a shock to the nervous system, even that of the murderer's."

Eustis's eyes were reflective. "The last thing I remember is sitting up in bed reading and listening to my tape recorder. And then for some reason I found myself on the floor beside Hermione with Oglethorpe shaking me awake." He stifled a yawn. "Very possibly I simply dozed off and fell out of bed."

"Nonsense," Oglethorpe said. "If you had fallen out of bed, surely your thud on the floor would have wakened you. And furthermore, you were at least twelve feet from the bed when I found you. Face it, Eustis, you shot Hermione and then fainted."

I turned to Genevieve. "You heard the shot?"

She nodded. "We were just outside their bedroom door. Oglethorpe and I had finished listening to the ten o'clock TV news and we were in the hallway going to our respective rooms when we heard the shot. We knocked at the door and asked if there was anything wrong, but we received no answer. We tried the doorknob, but the door was bolted."

"How did you get in?"

Oglethorpe touched his hearing aid for a moment. "We went through my bedroom out onto the balcony till we got to the French doors, but they were bolted from the inside."

Genevieve corroborated that. "Oglethorpe finally had to take one of the balcony chairs and break a glass pane in one of the doors. He reached inside and unbolted it."

"Are you positive that all of the French doors were bolted from the inside?"

"Positive," Genevieve said. "And the bedroom door to the hallway was bolted from the inside too."

I nodded thoughtfully. "You and your brother spent the evening watching television?"

"No," said Oglethorpe. "Frankly, I don't care for television except for the news programs. I was downstairs in my workshop turning table legs most of the evening."

I turned to Eustis. "Did you have a quarrel with your wife?"

He put his right hand over his heart. "We were happily married for nearly eight months. We never exchanged as much as a harsh word."

Genevieve reluctantly agreed. "Come to think of it, Eustis never *did* quarrel with Hermione. I think that's a little unnatural."

"If we should rule out murder as the result of a quarrel," I said, "would there be any other reason Mr. Crawford would want to murder his wife?"

Oglethorpe adjusted something on his hearing aid. "For her money, of course, Hermione was rather wealthy, in a lower-upper-class sort of way, and she kept Eustis on a strict allowance."

I drew Ralph to one side. "Well, Ralph, we've finally got one."

"Got one what?"

"A closed-room murder mystery."

"There's no mystery about it. Eustis shot his wife. He's the only one who could have done it. The room was locked from the inside."

"Exactly," I said. "But, Ralph, if Eustis was going to murder his wife — especially for money — would he have arranged to lock himself in the same room with her body?"

"All right, maybe it wasn't for money. They just had their first spat, he lost his temper, and shot her. Then he fainted."

"Ralph," I said. "This is a rather large house and it has many rooms. Doesn't it strike you as rather a coincidence that Oglethorpe and Genevieve should just happen to have been outside the door at the exact moment the shot was fired?"

We drew Genevieve Wesson to a private corner of the room. "You say your Aunt Hermione had quite a bit of money?" I asked.

"Quite a bit."

"And Eustis?"

"Nothing really. Eustis was the chief accountant at the Performing Arts Center. Hermione was on the Board of Sponsors and she met Eustis when she came to him to discuss the financial arrangements for an appearance of the Bulgarian National Ballet Company. One thing led to another and they were married."

"Ah," I said. "And after she married Eustis, did she not change her will so that he would get the major portion of her money in the event of her death?"

"Hermione never made out a will in her life. She was one of those people who believe they will die immediately if they do."

"If Hermione had died of natural causes, her husband would have gotten her estate?"

"I suppose that's what would have happened."

"However, your aunt did not die of natural causes, did she? And so if Eustis is convicted of her murder he cannot inherit any part of her estate, since a murderer may not profit from his crime."

Genevieve smiled. "I'm counting on that."

I returned to Eustis who had yawned again and now appeared to be looking for a place to sit down. "Could you give me your version of this unfortunate incident?"

He sighed. "Well, there really isn't much to tell. Hermione and I went upstairs at about ten. We usually read in bed for a while before turning out the light. The last thing I remember is reading Edgar Allan Poe's *The Purloined Letter* and listening to the *Pavane for a Dead Princess* on my tape recorder." He frowned in thought. "Or did I play *The Pines of Rome*? For some reason I keep confusing the two compositions."

"Mr. Crawford," I said, "do you take pills—I mean sleeping pills?"

"Goodness no. I have no trouble at all getting to sleep once I close my eyes."

"Before you and your wife went up to your room did you have anything to eat or drink?"

"I had a brandy and soda downstairs. I usually do before I go to sleep. It helps me to relax."

"Who made the drink for you?"

"I made it myself."

"Who owns the revolver used to kill your wife?"

"I really don't know. I never saw it before in my life."

Ralph and I took Eustis back to the bedroom where murder had been committed. I spoke to Dr. Tanner, the chief medic. "I'd like you to take a sample of this man's blood'"

Tanner nodded. "Am I supposed to look for anything in particular?"

"Barbiturates," I said. "Or anything in the sleep-inducing category."

I left Eustis with Tanner and took Ralph to one side. "We've got to examine this room thoroughly, Ralph. I want to be absolutely certain that this was indeed a locked chamber at the time of the murder. Search for any openings, no matter how small. Hot-air registers, bell ropes."

"Bell ropes?"

"Those things used for summoning servants. Snakes have been known to crawl up and down bell ropes and fatally bite people."

Ralph looked at the ceiling. "Well, now, Henry, snakes and bell ropes are tricky things. Personally, I think that if a snake started down from the top of a bell rope, he'd just lose his grip and flop down and maybe fracture a vertebra. And if he tried to get back up, I don't think he could make it either. Bell ropes are just too vertical, Henry. Now if you could find one that's off-center about forty-five degrees, maybe, just maybe —"

"Ralph," I said patiently, "why must you rattle on about the prehensility and gripping strength of vipers? Hermione Crawford was shot. Not bitten by a snake." I rubbed my hands. "Now let us examine the room for any apertures."

After fifteen minutes, we rejoined each other.

"Not one damn aperture, Henry. No bell ropes or hot-air registers. The room is heated by radiant baseboard. As far as I can see, this place was airtight when Hermione Crawford was shot and Eustis was alone with her when it happened."

"Ralph," I said, "look at this tape recorder on the nightstand."

He looked. "So?"

"It doesn't have any tape in it," I said.

"It's right next to the recorder, Henry."

"I know. But it shouldn't be." I inserted the tape, turned on the recorder, and listened. Was it *The Pines of Rome, The Pavane for a Dead Princess*? I shrugged and turned it off.

I went back to Eustis Crawford, who was now having his hands tested for the presence of gunpowder grains. "Mr. Crawford, you say that the last thing you remember is being in bed with your wife and reading while listening to your tape recorder?"

"Yes."

"Did you hear out the tape to the end and then remove it from the tape recorder?"

"No. I fell asleep while it was playing."

I left Eustis yawning and took Ralph to the French doors. "Look at this, Ralph. Each of these panes of glass is held in place by four small slats of wood." I pointed to the frame which had been broken to gain access to the room. "You will notice that there are some light scratches here, as though perhaps a screwdriver had been used to remove the slats at one time."

Ralph peered closer and said, "Hmm."

I nodded. "I must speculate to some degree, but I believe I have the answer to this entire riddle. We will start from the beginning. This evening someone in this household slipped barbiturates into Eustis Crawford's bottle of brandy. Unless the bottle was destroyed or hidden, I think that we'll find it in the liquor cabinet downstairs. And after consuming his drink, Eustis went upstairs with his wife."

Ralph rubbed his jaw. "And once they got inside, they bolted the bedroom door and also the French doors?"

"Not necessarily, Ralph, though it's possible. But they did get into bed and Eustis picked up a book and turned on his tape recorder. Meanwhile, the murderer waited somewhere out in the darkness of the balcony until he saw Eustis lapse into his drugged sleep."

"Murderer?"

"Or murderess. I will use the word murderer for convenience at the moment. And once Eustis was asleep, the murderer entered the room via the French doors. Or if they were bolted, all he had to do was tap on the glass to gain Hermione's attention, smile sweetly, and ask to be let cause he wanted to talk with her for a moment. And since the person she saw was either her nephew or her niece, she had no reason to suspect foul play. But when Hermione let him in, he produced the revolver and shot her.

"He then dragged the unconscious Eustis out of his bed and placed him beside his dead wife. He replaced the cartridge he had fired with another one and then formed Eustis's hand around the revolver. He fired the gun again, this time through the open French door and into the night. He did that so that we would be certain of finding gunpowder grains on Eustis's hand."

"How come nobody heard the shots, Henry?"

"Because the murderer used a silencer."

Ralph thought about it. "In that case, though, shouldn't the murderer have powder grains on his hand too?"

"I doubt it. If he knew enough about powder grains to put them on Eustis's hand, then surely he must have been intelligent enough to take pains that none of them appeared on his own person. Very likely he wore gloves and some other protective device to prevent the powder grains from getting on his hands or clothing."

I noticed that Eustis had fallen asleep in his chair. "And then the murderer removed the *Pavane for a Dead Princess* or whatever — from Eustis's tape recorder and substituted a tape of his own. This tape was entirely blank, except for the sound of one pistol shot."

Ralph raised an interested eyebrow.

I nodded. "Timing was incredibly important here."

He knew the precise moment the tape would reach the point of the shot, which would be within a minute or two of ten-forty. He turned on the recorder, with the volume undoubtedly high, and then bolted the bedroom door from the inside — if was not bolted already. And then, probably with a screwdriver, he removed one of the panes from a French door — the one which we now see broken.

"He stepped out onto the balcony, closed the door after him, reached back inside, and ran the bolt home. Then he replaced the windowpane and the slats, went down to the drawing room, and remained there listening to the ten o'clock news. At ten-thirty, as usual Oglethorpe and Genevieve went upstairs, putting them in the vicinity of Hermione's bedroom door at the moment the tape reached the sound of the shot. When the murderer gained access to the room from the balcony later, it was a simple matter to slip the tape back into his pocket — he has probably managed to dispose of it by now."

Ralph scratched his neck speculatively. "Who's your candidate for the murder? Oglethorpe or Genevieve?"

"Oglethorpe."

"Why Oglethorpe? "

"Because of the hearing aid."

"What does the hearing aid have to do with it?"

" I haven't quite pinpointed that yet, but it's probably the key to this entire case. Every time I've looked at Oglethorpe, he's been fiddling with that hearing aid. That's got to be significant somehow."

"Why? . . ."

"Ralph, I said, "do you remember the Gillginham murder case? One of our prime suspects, Elmer Bjornson, appeared to be confined to a wheelchair, but we discovered that he could really walk. That taught me to always be suspicious of murder suspects in wheelchairs and by extension I think I can safely apply that to people who wear hearing aids."

"Henry," Ralph said, "it's true that Bjornson could walk, but that didn't have anything to do with the murder of Gillingham. We just stumbled across that before we arrested the real murderer."

I rubbed my jaw. "You mean that Oglethorpe's hearing aid has *nothing* to do with this murder?"

"I'm afraid not, Henry."

I pulled myself together. "Ah well, nailing the true murderer in this case is just a matter of perseverance to come up with the culprit or culpritess soon. But at least for the time being, we have succeeded in preventing an innocent man from being sent to prison." I smiled modestly. "Actually, I suppose almost any reasonably competent detective would eventually have come up with all the glaring inconsistencies in this case."

Ralph nodded. "That's right, Henry."

There was a rather long silence and I began to feel uneasy. "What is it, Ralph?"

He sighed. "This case reminds me of the purloined letter."

"How does it remind you of the purloined letter?"

"Henry, the best place to hide a murder is inside a murder. Suppose you want to kill your wife for her money. No matter how cleverly you plan the thing, you know that you will still be the most logical suspect. The police would dig and dig and the chances are good that they would come up with something that would trip you up. So you decide to take the bull by the horns. Since you are going to be suspected anyway, why not go all out? Make it seem at first glance that only you could possibly have killed her."

I closed my eyes.

Ralph continued. "When you go upstairs with your wife you shoot her, using a silencer on the gun. Then you leave the room and get rid of (he silencer and the spent cartridge and replace it with a fresh one. You return to the room, wait until you hear Oglethorpe and Genevieve coming up the stairs. You let them get just outside the door and then you fire the pistol out of the open French door into the night air.

"And while Oglethorpe and Genevieve are knocking at the bedroom door, you simply close and bolt the French doors— one of whose window frames you have previous tampered with. Then you swallow a few barbiturates and lie beside your dead wife. You pretend that you are unconscious when Genevieve and Oglethorpe break into the room and that is that."

Ralph sighed again. "You then sit back and let the police do their work. They will realize that the situation is just *too* pat, *too* overwhelming. Point by point, they will unravel the frame-up and feel noble while they are doing it. Even if, by some remote chance, you are actually brought to trial, any good lawyer could point out the holes in the case and get you an acquittal."

I stared at Eustis, asleep in his chair with a smile on his face.

Damn, I thought, *Ralph's right. And he's going to get away with it.*

We carried Eustis to headquarters, but without any great optimism.

Then Ralph and I dropped in at the nearest tavern.

The bartender recognized me. "What'll it be, sergeant? Tomato juice or sherry?"

"Sherry."

"Oh," he said. "That bad a day?"

I nodded glumly. "That bad a day."

He filled my glass to the brim and gave me water for a chaser.

The Crime Machine

"I was present the last time you committed murder," Henry said.

I lit my cigar. "Really?"

"Of course you couldn't see me."

I smiled. "You were in your time machine?"

Henry nodded.

Naturally I didn't believe a word of it. About the time machine. He *could* actually have been present however, but not in that fantastic manner.

Murder is my business and the fact that there had been a witness when I disposed of James Grady was naturally disconcerting. And now, for the sake of security, I would have to devise some means of getting rid of Henry. I had no intention of being blackmailed by him. Not for any length of time, at least.

"I must warn you that I have taken pains to let people know that I have come here, Mr. Reeves," Henry said. "They do not know why I am here, but they do know that I am here. You understand, don't you?"

I smiled again. "I do not murder people in my own apartment. It is the height of inhospitality. And so there will be no necessity for you to switch our drinks. I assure you your glass contains nothing stronger than brandy."

The situation was basically unpleasant, but nevertheless I found myself rather enjoying Henry's bizarre story. "This machine of yours, Henry, is it a bit like a barber's chair?"

"To some degree," he admitted. "Evidently we had both seen the same motion picture. With a round reflector-like device behind you? And levers in front which you pull to propel you into the past? Or the future?"

"Just the past. I'm still working on the mechanism for the future." Henry sipped his brandy. "My machine is also mobile. That is, it not only projects me into the past, but also to any point on the earth I desire."

Excellent, I thought. Quite an improvement over the old model time machines. "And you are invisible?"

"Correct. I cannot participate in any manner in the past. I can only observe."

This madman did at least think with some degree of logic. To so much as injure the wing of a butterfly ten thousand years ago could conceivably re-shuffle the course of history.

Henry had come to my apartment at three in the afternoon. He had not given me his last name, which was entirely natural since he intended to blackmail me. He was fairly tall and thin, with glasses that gave him an owlish appearance and hair that tended toward anarchy.

He leaned forward. "I read in yesterday's newspaper that a James Grady was shot to death in a warehouse on Blenheim Street at approximately eleven in the evening of July the twenty-seventh."

I thought I could supply the rest. "And so you hopped into your time machine, set the dials back to July the twenty-seventh and to Blenheim Street and were there at ten-thirty for a ringside seat, waiting for me to re-commit the crime?"

"Precisely."

I would have to discuss this particular form of insanity with Dr. Powers. He is a quite mature and—since I disposed of his wife—wealthy psychiatrist.

Henry smiled thinly. "You shot James Grady at exactly ten fifty-one. As you stooped over him to make certain that he was dead, you dropped your car keys. You said, 'Oh, damn!' and picked them up. At the door of the warehouse, you looked back and lifted your hand in a mock salute to the corpse. Then you departed."

Unquestionably he had been there. Not in that fabulous time machine, but probably hiding among the thousands of boxes and bales inside the warehouse—an accidental witness to the murder. It was one of those unfortunate coincidences that occur occasionally to mar an otherwise perfect killing. But why did he bother to resort to this fantastic story?

Henry put down his glass. "I think that five thousand dollars would be sufficient for me to forget what I saw."

For how long, I wondered. A month? Two? I took a puff of my cigar. "If you went to the police, it would be your word against mine."

"Could you bear an investigation?"

I really didn't know. I am a very careful practitioner of my craft, but it was still possible that here and there I might have made some slight revealing error. I certainly would not welcome the interest of the authorities. Of that much I was positive.

I replenished my glass. "You seem to have fallen into an interesting and profitable business. Have you approached many other murderers?" I looked at his suit. It had undoubtedly been sold with two pairs of trousers.

Perhaps he read my mind. "I have just started, Mr. Reeves. You are the first murderer I have approached."

He smiled primly. "I have done considerable other research on you, Mr. Reeves. On June the tenth, at eleven-twelve in the evening, an automobile which you had stolen for the purpose ran down a Mrs. Irvin Perry."

He could have read about Mrs. Perry's death in the newspapers. But how did he know that I had been the driver? A wild guess?

"You parked approximately one hundred yards from the intersection.

You kept your motor running while you waited for Mrs. Perry to make her appearance. Ten minutes before she arrived, a collie ran across the street. Seven minutes before she arrived, a fire engine sped past. Three minutes before she arrived, a Model A Ford filled with teenagers raced by. The automobile's muffler was faulty. It was quite noisy."

I frowned. How could he possibly have known those things?

Henry was enjoying himself. "On September twenty-eighth, at two-fifteen of a chilly afternoon, a Gerald Mitchell 'fell' off an escarpment near his home while he was taking a stroll. You had a bit of trouble with him. Though he was a small man, he showed remarkable strength. He managed to tear the left pocket of your coat before you could throw him into space."

I caught myself staring at him and quickly took a sip of brandy.

"Five thousand dollars," Henry said. "Small bills, of course. Nothing larger than a five hundred. Naturally I didn't expect you to have that much cash lying about. I shall return tomorrow evening at eight."

I pulled myself together. For a moment I had almost entertained the thought that Henry actually might have a time machine. But there was some other explanation and I would have to think it out.

At the door to the hallway, I smiled. "Henry, would you hop into your time machine and find out who Jack the Ripper really was? I'm frightfully curious."

Henry nodded. "I'll do that tonight."

I closed the door and went into my living room.

My wife Diana put aside her fashion magazine. "Who was that strange creature?"

"He claims to be an inventor."

"Really? He certainly looks mad enough for the part. I imagine he wanted to sell you an invention?"

"Not exactly."

Diana is green-eyed and cool and she is perhaps no more predatory or unfaithful than any other woman who marries a man with money who is thirty years her senior. I am fully aware of the nature of our relationship, but I realize that one must pay by various means for the enjoyment of a work of art. And Diana is a work of art—a triumph of physical nature. I value her quite as highly as I do my Modiglianis and my Van Goghs.

"What is he supposed to have invented?"

"A time machine."

She smiled. "I am partial to perpetual motion machines."

I was faintly irritated. "Perhaps it works."

She studied me. "I hope you have no intention of letting that strange man talk you out of money."

"No, my dear. I still retain my mental faculties."

Her solicitude for my money would have been touching, except that I realized that she preferred to spend it on herself. Henry's chances of acquiring any of it were nil as far as she was concerned.

She picked up the magazine. "Has he asked you to see it?"

"No. And even if he does, I have no intention of doing so,"

And yet I wondered how Henry could possibly have managed to know the details of those three murders. His presence at one of them could be an acceptable coincidence. But three?

There was no such a thing as a time machine. There had to be some other explanation—something that an intelligent man could believe.

I glanced at my watch and turned my mind to another subject.

"I have something to attend to, Diana. I'll be back in an hour or two."

I drove to the main post office downtown and opened my box with a key. The letter I had been expecting was inside.

I conduct most of my business by mail and box number. My clients do not know my name, even on those occasions when personal contact is necessary.

The letter was from Jason Spender. We had exchanged some correspondence and Spender had been negotiating for the elimination of a Charles Atwood. Spender did not give his reasons for that desire and for my purposes they were not necessary. In this case, however, I could hazard a guess. Spender and Atwood were partners in a building concern and evidently sharing the profits no longer appealed to Spender.

The letter accepted my terms—fifteen thousand dollars —and provided the information that Atwood had a dinner engagement tomorrow evening and would return to his home at approximately eleven. Spender would have an alibi for that particular time in the event that the police might make embarrassing inquiries.

I drove on to the Shippler Detective Agency and went directly to Andrew Shippler.

I cannot, of course, employ his agency continuously to follow my wife. But several times a year I made a precautionary use of his services for a week or two. It is usually sufficient.

In 1958, for instance, Shippler discovered a Terence Reilly. He was extremely personable—fair, athletic, and the type to which Diana seems to be drawn—and I cannot blame Diana too much.

However Terence Reilly soon departed this world. I was not paid for the demise. It was a labor of love.

Shippler was a plump man in his fifties with the air of an accountant. He took a typewritten page from a folder and adjusted his rimless glasses. "Your wife left your apartment twice yesterday. In the morning at ten-thirty she went to a small hat shop for an hour. She finally purchased a blue and white hat with . . .

"Never mind the details."

He was slightly aggrieved. "But details can be important, Mr. Reeves. We try to be absolutely thorough." He glanced at the page again. "Then she had a strawberry soda at a drugstore and went on to . . ."

I interrupted again. "Did she see anyone? Talk to anyone?"

"Well, the owner of the hat shop and the clerk at the drugstore counter."

"Besides that," I snapped.

He shook his head. "No. But she left the apartment again at two-thirty in the afternoon. She went to a small cocktail bar on Farwell. There she met two women her age, apparently by prearrangement. It appears that they had been college classmates and hadn't seen each other for years. My man overheard most of their conversation. They discussed their former classmates and what they were doing now." Shippler cleared his throat. "It seems that they were most impressed that your wife had . . . ah . . . caught such a man of means."

"What did Diana say?"

"She was extremely noncommittal." Shippler folded his hands. "Your wife consumed one Pink Lady and one Manhattan during the course of two hours."

"I am not interested in my wife's liquor preferences. Did she see anyone else? A man?"

Shippler shook his head. "No. At four-ten she left the two women and returned to your apartment."

The human mind is a peculiar thing. I was relieved, of course—and yet, a trifle disappointed.

"Shall we keep watching her?" Shippler asked hopefully.

This time I had had Diana under a surveillance for about a week. I mulled over Shippler's question. Shippler charged one hundred dollars a day and that was rather expensive. I smiled slightly. Now if I had Henry's time machine, I could save a great deal of money. "Watch her a few days more," I said. "And I have something else for you."

"Yes?"

"At eight tomorrow evening, I am expecting a caller. He will be with me ten to twenty minutes. When he leaves, I want him followed. I want to know who he is and where he lives." I gave Shippler a description of Henry. "Phone me as soon as you find out."

I went to the bank and withdrew five thousand dollars.

At seven the next evening Diana left to see a motion picture. Or at least so she informed me. I would find out about that later.

Henry arrived punctually at eight o'clock and I took him into my study.

He took a chair. "He was a clerk with an importing concern."

"Who was?" I asked.

"Jack the Ripper. A timid-looking man—in his early forties, I'd estimate. He was apparently a bachelor and he lived with his mother."

I smiled. "How interesting. What was his name?"

"I haven't gotten that yet. You see, people don't go about with signs hanging from their necks and it can be difficult to find out who they actually are."

He could easily have invented some name for this Jack the Ripper, but this was really more clever—and logical.

Henry said, "Do you have the five thousand dollars?"

"Yes." I got the package and handed it to him.

He rose. "Tonight I think I'll go back to Custer's massacre. I find history fascinating."

I had only one consolation. When the time came to kill him, I would enjoy every moment of it.

When he was gone, I sat beside the phone and waited impatiently. At nine-thirty it rang and I quickly lifted the receiver.

"This is Shippler."

"Well, where does he live?"

Shippler's voice was apologetic. "I'm afraid my man lost him."

"What?"

"He transferred from bus to bus and finally disappeared.

I think he suspected he was being followed."

"You blundering idiot!" I roared.

"Really, Mr. Reeves," Shippler said stiffly. "It is my man who is the blundering idiot."

I hung up and poured myself some bourbon. This time Henry had eluded me, but there would be other times. He would be back. Blackmailers are never satisfied.

I became aware of the time and realized that I still had work to do that night. I got into my coat and hat and went downstairs to the apartment garage.

Charles Atwood's home was a large one embedded in several acres of wooded property. It was a situation I fancied, since it offered the maximum of concealment.

The dwelling was dark, except for lights on the third floor where I imagined the servants were quartered.

Atwood's three-car garage was detached from the house. I took a stand behind a clump of trees near it and waited.

At eleven-fifteen a car swung into the driveway and made its way to the garage. It stopped momentarily while the automatic doors rose, and then it disappeared into the garage.

Thirty seconds later, a side door opened and a tall man stepped into the moonlight. He began walking toward the house.

I had my revolver and silencer ready and I waited until he came within fifteen feet of me before I left my concealment.

Atwood stopped with an exclamation of startled surprise as he saw me.

I pulled the trigger and Atwood dropped to the ground without a sound. I made certain that he was dead—I do not like to leave things half done—and then made my way back through the woods and to the street where I had parked my car.

The assignment had been entirely successful and, for the first time in thirty-six hours, I felt a certain peace with the world.

I returned to my apartment a little before midnight and I was relaxing when the phone shrilled.

It was Henry. "I see that you killed someone else tonight," he announced pleasantly.

My hands were moist.

"When I arrived home," Henry said, "I got into my time machine and turned it back to the time when I left your apartment. I wanted to see if you had attempted to follow me. I have to be cautious, you know. After all, I am dealing with a murderer."

I said nothing.

"You didn't follow me, but you did leave your apartment and I followed in my machine as a matter of curiosity."

That infernal time machine! Was it possible?

"I'm just wondering," Henry said. "Was that the man you were supposed to kill—the one you killed?"

What was he getting at?

"Because there were two men in the car," Henry said.

I spoke involuntarily. "Two?"

"Yes. You shot the first man as he came out of the garage. The second man left it about forty-five seconds later."

I closed my eyes. "Did he see me?"

"No. You were gone by that time. He just bent over the man you'd shot and called, 'Fred! Fred!'"

I was definitely perspiring. "Henry, I'd like to see you."

"Why?"

"I can't discuss it over the phone. But I've got to see you."

His voice was dubious. "I don't know."

"It means money. A lot of money."

He thought it over. "All right," he said finally. "Tomorrow? Around eight?"

I couldn't wait that long. "No. Right now. As soon as you can get here."

Henry required more seconds to think. "No tricks now, Mr. Reeves," he said. "Be prepared for anything."

"No tricks, Henry. I swear it. Get here as soon as you can."

He arrived forty-five minutes later. "What is it, Mr. Reeves?"

I had been drinking—not to excess, but I simply found that accepting such an idea—and I was on the verge of accepting it—was painful to my intelligence. "Henry, I'd like to buy your machine. If it really works."

"It works." He shook his head. "But I won't sell it."

"One hundred thousand dollars, Henry."

"Out of the question."

"A hundred and fifty thousand."

"It's my invention," Henry said peevishly. "I wouldn't dream of parting with it."

"You could make another, couldn't you?"

"Well . . . yes." He eyed me suspiciously.

"Henry, do you expect me to mass produce time machines once I get yours? To sell them to others?"

His face indicated that evidently he did.

"Henry," I said patiently. "Having anyone else in the world get hold of that machine is the last thing I want. After all, I am a murderer. I wouldn't welcome other people delving into the past, especially my past—now would I?"

"No," he admitted. "Somebody else might want to turn you over to the police. There are people like that."

"Two hundred thousand dollars, Henry," I said. "My last offer." Actually money was no object to me now. With Henry's machine—if it worked—I could make millions.

A crafty light crept into his eyes. "Two hundred and fifty thousand. Take it or leave it."

"Henry, you drive a hard bargain. But I'll meet your price. However I've got to be satisfied that the machine works. When can I see it?"

"I'll get in touch with you," he said cagily. "Tomorrow, the next day, maybe in a week."

"Why not right now?"

He shook his head. "No. You're very clever, Mr. Reeves. Perhaps you've devised a trap for this moment. I prefer to set the time and terms myself."

I was unable to shake him out of his determination and he left five minutes later.

I rose at seven in the morning and went downstairs to purchase a newspaper. I had indeed killed the wrong man. A Fred Turley. I had never even heard of him before.

Atwood and Turley had returned from the dinner and an evening of cards together and driven into the garage. Turley had gone out of the side door, but Atwood remained behind to lock his car. Then he had seen his briefcase still on the rear seat. After he had recovered it, relocked the car, and left the garage, he had found Turley dead on the path leading to the house. At first he had thought Turley had suffered a stroke of some kind. When he finally discovered the truth, he had raised an alarm. The police had no clues either to the identity of the murderer or the motive for the killing.

I found myself fretting about the apartment all morning waiting for Henry to phone me. I skimmed through the paper a half a dozen times before an item in the local section caught my eye.

It seemed that once again some fool had bought a "money machine."

This form of swindle was probably as old as currency itself. The victim was approached by a stranger claiming to have a money machine. One simply inserted a dollar, turned the handle, and a twenty dollar bill emerged from the opposite end. In this case, the victim had purchased the machine for five hundred dollars—the stranger claiming that he was forced to sell because he needed cash.

People are incredible idiots!

Couldn't the victim have the basic intelligence and imagination to realize that if the machine were actually genuine, all that the stranger had to do to get five hundred dollars himself was to turn the handle twenty-five times and transform twenty-five dollars into five hundred?

Yes, people are monumental . . .

I found myself reading the article again. Then I went to the liquor cabinet. After two bourbons, I allowed myself to bask in the returning sun of sanity.

I had almost fallen into Henry's trap. I had, I reluctantly admitted, been just a bit stupid.

I smiled. Still . . . it might be a rather amusing adventure to see Henry's time machine—to see in what manner he hoped to convince me that it actually worked.

Henry came to my apartment at one o'clock in the afternoon. He appeared shaken. "Horrible," he muttered. "Horrible."

"What's horrible?"

"Custer's massacre." He wiped his forehead with a handkerchief. "I'll have to avoid things like that in the future."

I almost laughed. Rather a neat touch. Henry knew how to act. "And now we see your machine?"

Henry nodded. "I suppose so. We'll take your car. Mine's in the garage for repairs."

I had driven him about a mile, when he told me to pull over to the curb. I glanced about "Is this where you live?"

"No. But from here on I drive your car. You will be blindfolded and you will lie on the back seat."

"Oh, come now, Henry!"

"It's absolutely necessary if you want me to take you to the machine," Henry said stubbornly. "And I've got to search you to see that you aren't carrying a weapon."

I was not carrying a weapon and Henry's idea of a blindfold consisted of a black hood that fitted over my entire head and was fastened by strings at the back of the neck.

"I'll be keeping an eye on you through the rearview mirror," Henry cautioned. "If I see you touch that blindfold the whole thing is off."

Automatically I found myself trying to remember the turns Henry made as he drove and attempting to identify sounds which might tell me where he was taking me. However, the task proved too complicated and I finally relaxed as much as I could and waited for the drive to end.

After an hour, the car finally slowed to a stop. Henry left the wheel and I heard what I believed to be the sound of garage doors being opened. Henry returned to the car; we moved forward fifteen feet or so, and stopped again.

The doors were closed and I heard a light switch flicked on.

"We're here," Henry said. "I'll take off that blindfold now."

As I had surmised, we were in a garage—but plywood sheets had been nailed over all the windows and a single electric light burned overhead. A stout oak door was in the cement building-block wall to the left.

Henry produced a revolver.

A horrendous thought gripped me. What a fool I had been! I had blindly—literally and figuratively—allowed myself to be lured here. And now, for reasons unknown to me, Henry was about to kill me!

"Henry," I began, "I'm sure we can talk this over and come to some . . ."

He waved the gun. "This is just a precaution. In case you have any ideas."

I was too uneasy to have any ideas.

Henry produced a key and went to the oak door. "This used to be a two-car garage, but I divided it in half. The time machine is in here." He unlocked the door and switched on an overhead light.

Henry's time machine was just about as I had anticipated—a metallic chair with some scant leather upholstering, a large mirror-bright aluminum shield or reflector behind it, and a series of levers, dials, and buttons on a control board attached to the platform on which the chair stood.

The room was windowless and all four walls—with the exception of three grated ventilators approximately shoulder high—were solid cement block. The floor was concrete and the ceiling was plastered.

I smiled. "Henry, your machine looks almost like an electric chair."

"Yes," he said musingly, "it does look rather like that, doesn't it?"

I stared at him. Could he have been so insidious as to actually . . . I studied the machine again. "Naturally I want a demonstration. How does it work?"

"Get into the chair and I'll show you which levers to pull."

The device *did* look a great deal like an electric chair. I cleared my throat. "I have a better idea, Henry. Suppose you take a trip in the chair. I'll just wait right here until you return."

Henry gave it a thought. "All right. But you'll have to leave the room."

Ah ha, I thought.

"You see when I start the machine," Henry said, "it creates quite a disturbance around me. That's why I had to make this room so solid. I've installed ventilators to take care of some of the turbulence, but I'm not too sure how well they work. I have no idea what might happen to you if you remained."

I smiled. "I might possibly be injured? Or killed?"

"Exactly. So if you'll leave and close the door I'll get on with it. And another precaution. When I return, you've got to be out of the room, too."

I chuckled to myself as I left and closed the door behind me. I lit a cigar and waited, amused.

What happened next was most impressive. First there was a low whine, as though a generator were starting. It rose gradually in pitch and then came a rumbling sound mixed with the undulating keen of a fierce wind. It increased in volume and lasted for approximately a minute.

Then it stopped abruptly and there was absolute silence.

Yes, I thought. Altogether a good show. But then it would have to be if Henry expected to extract two hundred and fifty thousand dollars from me.

I went to the door and opened it.

The room was empty!

I stood there gaping. It couldn't be! The only way out of the room was the door I had just entered and even that was certainly too small to pull the chair through. And the only other openings were the three grated ventilators and they were less than two feet square!

The whining suddenly rose again. Strong air currents swirled around the room and I found myself gasping as I fled the room and slammed the door behind me.

The noise became deafening and then, just as abruptly as before, it stopped.

The door clicked open and Henry stepped out of the room. Behind him I could see the time machine back in its place.

Henry appeared thoughtful. Finally he shook his head. "Cleopatra wasn't even good-looking."

My heart was still pounding. "You were gone only a minute or two."

He waved a hand. "In one time sense. Actually I spent an hour on her barge." He came back to the present. "You can raise two hundred and fifty thousand dollars?"

I nodded weakly. "It will take a week or two." I wiped my forehead. "Henry, I've got to take a trip on that chair." Henry frowned. "I've been thinking that over, Mr.

Reeves. No. You could steal my invention."

"But how? Wouldn't I have to come back here?"

"No. You could go into the past and then return to any place in the world. Perhaps a thousand miles from here."

He pulled a small wrench from his pocket and began disconnecting a section of the control panel.

"What are you doing?"

"I'm taking out some key transistors. I think I'll keep them on my person. That way if someone should steal my time machine he would find it useless."

Henry drove me back to my apartment, taking the same precautions as before, and then he left me.

In America we seem to have a feeling of guilt about discarding old license plates and Henry had been no exception. There had been four old sets of them nailed to the garage wall and I had memorized two of them.

I got Shippler on the phone. "Can you trace license numbers?"

"Yes, Mr. Reeves. I have a connection at the state capitol."

I gave him the numbers. "The first is a 1958 license number and the second is 1959. I want the name and address of the owner as soon as possible. Phone me the moment you get the information."

I was about to hang up.

"Oh, Mr. Reeves. We have the report on your wife for yesterday. Would you like me to give it over the phone?"

I had forgotten about that. "Well?"

"She left the apartment yesterday morning at ten-thirty. She bought some orange sticks and nail polish at the drugstore."

"What shade of nail polish?" I asked dryly.

"Summer Rose," he said proudly. "Then she went to—"

"Never mind all that. Did she meet anyone?"

"No, sir. Just the drugstore clerk. A woman. But in the evening she again left your apartment at three minutes after seven. She met a woman named Doris. My man overheard Doris say that she has twins."

I sighed.

"They went to a show and left at eleven-thirty."

I was not going to ask him the name of the picture. "Is that all?"

"Yes, sir. She returned to your apartment at eleven-fifty-six. The name of the picture . . ."

I hung up and made myself a whiskey and soda.

The idea of a time machine was fantastic. But was it really? We are all aware that there is a fourth dimension. And future travelers in space will eventually have to use space warp in order to reach planets that are physically inaccessible in the present time sense.

Diana came into the room with a manicure kit. "You look thoughtful."

"I have a lot to think about."

"Does it have anything to do with that man who was here? The inventor?"

I sipped my whiskey. "Suppose I told you that his time machine works?"

She began working on her nails. "I hope you haven't been taken in?"

I noticed that one of the bottles beside her was named Summer Rose. "And why should a time machine be impossible?"

"Don't tell me he's convinced you?"

I felt a bit defensive. "Perhaps."

She smiled. "Has he asked you for money?"

I watched her use nail polish remover. "How much do you think a time machine would be worth?"

She raised an eyebrow.

I held up a hand. "Let us just *suppose* that there is such a thing? How much would *you* be willing to pay for it?"

She examined her nails. "Perhaps a thousand or two. It might be an amusing toy."

"A *toy?*" I laughed. "My dear, don't you realize the tremendous import of such a thing? You could go into the past and ferret out any secret at all."

She glanced up. "Perhaps try simple blackmail?"

"My dear Diana, not *simple* blackmail, but blackmail extended, doubled, quadrupled. No nation's secrets would be safe from discovery. You could sell your services to the government . . . any government . . . for millions. You could be present at the most important council chambers, the most isolated laboratories. . . ."

She looked up again. "Is that what you'd do if you had such a machine, use it for blackmail?"

I had let myself get carried away. I smiled. "Just indulging in fantasy, dear."

Her eyes seemed to calculate me. "Don't do anything foolish."

"My dear, I am the most cautious man in the world."

I decided that I would not hear from Shippler within the next half an hour and so I went to the post office.

I had a letter from Spender. He expressed keen disappointment that I had killed Turley instead of Atwood. He had played golf with Turley a number of times and would miss him. He also suggested that I return the fifteen thousand dollars or complete my assignment.

Shippler phoned at three-thirty.

"Both of the license numbers belong to the same person," he said. "A Henry Pruitt. He lives at 2349 West Headley. This city."

I waited until ten that evening and then got my flashlight, a tape measure, and my ring of special keys from the wall safe and went down to my car.

Henry's house was in a sparsely populated section of the city—there were empty lots on either side of his home. It was a two-story building, but still relatively small. A garage stood next to the alley.

I parked my car a hundred feet down the street and lit a cigar. At eleven the lights in the living room went out and a few moments later they reappeared in what was evidently an upstairs bedroom.

After ten minutes, they too went out.

I waited another half an hour and then made my way through the littered lots to the garage. It had originally been a common two-car structure, but now the left-hand doors had been replaced by a solid cement block wall. I couldn't peer into the right-hand unit, because, as I'd noticed before, the windows had been covered by plywood. Henry clearly believed in absolute secrecy for his invention.

I measured the outside of the garage, the height, width, and length. Then I took the ring of keys out of my pocket and, after a few tries, succeeded in opening the door. I stepped inside, closed the door behind me, and turned on my flashlight.

Yes, this was the place I had been in earlier in the day—the four pairs of license plates nailed to the wall, the workbench at the far end, and the door leading to the time machine on the left.

I switched on the overhead light.

The door to the next room was also locked, but it presented no problem to me. I turned on the light, somewhat apprehensively.

Yes, there it was. The time machine!

For a moment, the idea of stealing it crossed my mind. But then I remembered that Henry had a section of the controls. And besides, how would I get it out of the room? The doorway was obviously too small.

For that matter, how had Henry gotten the machine *into* the room?

I pondered on that and decided he must have brought it in piecemeal and then assembled it.

What really concerned me was how he had managed, earlier in the day, to get the time machine *out* of the room.

That was what I was there to find out.

I began by examining the walls. They were cement block on all four sides and absolutely solid. I took measurements of the room and the entire inside of the garage. My computations showed that there were no secret compartments, no false chambers. I examined the ventilator grates thoroughly. I tried to shake them loose, but they were securely screwed into place. They could not be removed without some time and effort. I examined the floor. It was compact and unbroken cement.

There was one more possibility. The ceiling. Perhaps Henry had some device—some series of hoists—that would whisk the machine into a ceiling crevice.

I got a step ladder from the other room and went over the ceiling with minute thoroughness. The plaster was old and a bit grimy, but there was not even one crack that might indicate access to some secret compartment above.

I got off the ladder and found myself trembling.

There was no possible way out of this room. None at all.

Except by the time machine!

It was ten minutes before the weakness left me. I turned out the lights and locked both doors behind me.

The next morning I began converting my capital into cash.

Shippler called in the afternoon with his daily report: "Mrs. Reeves attended a card party at the home of this Doris at two yesterday afternoon. I found out her last name. It's Weaver. The names of the twins are . . ."

"Confound it, I don't care what the names of the blasted twins are."

"Sorry. Your wife left there at four-thirty-six. She stopped at a super-market and bought four lamb chops, two pounds of—"

"She went shopping for the cook," I stormed. "Now do you have anything important?"

"Nothing really important, I guess."

"Then send me your bill. I won't be needing you anymore."

"Well, if you do," Shippler said brightly, "you know where we are. And congratulations."

"Congratulations? On what?"

"Well . . . on your wife's . . . ah . . . faithfulness . . . this time."

I hung up.

No. I wouldn't be needing Shippler any more. If I wanted to find out anything at all about Diana, I would soon be able to do so myself.

My thoughts went to Henry. He could undoubtedly build another time machine, but I couldn't allow that. In order for my plans to be effective I had to have a monopoly. Henry would have to go and I would see to that after I possessed the machine.

At the end of the week, I had the two hundred and fifty thousand dollars in cash. I was tempted to phone Henry, but I was afraid he might shy away entirely if he knew that I had discovered his identity.

Three excruciatingly long days more went by before Henry rang the door bell of my apartment.

I drew him quickly inside. "I have the money. All of it"

Henry rubbed an ear. "I really don't know whether I should sell the machine."

I glared at him. "Two hundred and fifty thousand dollars. It's all the money I have in the world. I won't pay another cent."

"It isn't the money. I just don't know if I ought to go through with it."

I opened the suitcase. "Look at it, Henry. Two hundred and fifty thousand dollars. Do you know what that much money can buy? You can make yourself dozens of time machines. You can gold-plate them. You can set jewels in them."

He still held back.

"Henry," I said severely. "We made a bargain, didn't we? You can't go back on that."

Henry finally sighed. "I suppose not. But I still think I'm making a mistake."

I rubbed my hands. "Now let's get down to my car. You may blindfold me and drive me to your place."

"Blindfolding won't be necessary now," Henry said morosely. "As long as you're getting the time machine you'll be able to find out who I am and where I live anyway."

How true. Henry was doomed.

"But I will search you," Henry said.

The ride to Henry's garage seemed interminable, but at last we were inside. Henry fumbled with the keys to the next room and I almost yielded to the urge to snatch them from him and do the job myself.

Finally he had the door open and switched on the overhead light.

The machine was there. Beautiful. Shining. And now it was mine.

Henry took the vital control unit out of his pocket and threaded it into place. He took a sheet of paper from his breast pocket. "These are the directions. Don't lose this paper or you might become stranded somewhere in time. Better yet, memorize them."

I took the sheet out of his hands.

"You may not get the exact date you want at the first try," Henry said. "Because calendars have been changed and besides, once you get back more than five hundred years, you'll find all sorts of errors in history. But you can approximate the time and then use this fine tuner over here in order to pinpoint . . ."

"Stop your babbling and get out of here!" I snapped. "I can read directions as well as anyone."

Henry was a bit miffed, but he left the room and closed the door.

I got into the chair and read the typewritten directions. They were absurdly simple. But I read them again and then put the paper in my pocket.

Now, where would I go?

I studied the controls.

Yes. I had it. The New Year's Eve party at the Lowells. Diana had disappeared at ten-thirty and I hadn't seen her again until two a.m. of January first, 1960. She had never given me a satisfactory explanation for her absence.

I adjusted the time control and the direction knob. I did not know the exact distance to the Lowells from this point, but I would use the fine tuner directly under the mileage dial once I got underway.

I hesitated a moment, took a deep breath, and then pressed the red button.

I waited.

Nothing happened.

I frowned and pressed the button again.

Nothing.

I took the slip out of my pocket and feverishly reviewed the directions. I had committed no errors.

And then I knew! The entire thing had been a hoax!

I leaped out of the chair and rushed to the door.

It was locked.

I pounded with my fists and called Henry's name. I cursed and shrieked until my voice was hoarse.

The door remained closed.

I managed to get some control over myself and darted to the time machine. I wrenched loose a section of the chair piping and returned to the door.

The piece of pipe was aluminum and fiendishly light and malleable. It took me more than forty-five minutes before I managed to force the pins out of the door hinges and get out of the room.

I found an envelope under the windshield wiper of my car and tore it open.

The typewritten pages were, of course, intended for *me*.

My dear Mr. Reeves:

Yes, you have been thoroughly hoaxed. There is no such a thing as a time machine.

I suppose I could leave it at that and allow you to go mad attempting to arrive at some reasonable explanation, but I shall not. I am quite proud of my little project and would like the attention of a truly appreciative audience.

I think you will do nicely.

How did I manage to know those interesting details of your last four murders?

I was there.

Not in the time machine, of course.

You are undoubtedly aware that it was not your urbanity, your charm, which attracted Diana to your hearth. She married you for your money—of which you gave indications of having a lot.

But you were extremely reticent about the extent and source of your wealth—an evasion which unquestionably can drive a woman to desperate curiosity. Especially a woman like Diana.

She had you followed and for the purpose employed a detective agency. Shippler, I believe the name was. They are quite thorough and I recommend them highly.

It was indeed fortunate for you—and certainly now for Diana and me—that you did not choose that particular time to commit one of your murders. But it was during one of your periods of unemployment and you were not followed for long. A week.

The reports concerning your activities were mundane, but Diana did fasten on one particular repeated detail they contained. And details are so important.

Every day you went to a rented box at the main post office.

Now why would you want a private box? Diana wondered. After all, you do have a home address and that should be sufficient for ordinary mail. Ordinary mail. That was it. This wasn't for ordinary mail.

It was child's play for Diana to get an impression of your box key while you slept and to have a duplicate made, for her use.

She made it a practice to go to your post office box each morning—you go there in the afternoon. Whenever she found a letter, she removed it, steamed it open, read the contents, and returned it to the box in plenty of time for you to pick it up the same day.

And so you see it was possible for her to know the details of your negotiations to murder, when the murders were scheduled to be committed and the places where they were to occur. And that made it possible for me to be there early, conceal myself, and *watch* you work.

Yes, we've known each other for some time—meeting discreetly—very discreetly. Diana remembers a Terence Reilly and his sudden disappearance. And as an added precaution—since we were on the verge of acquiring a quarter of a million dollars and wanted nothing to prevent that—we have not seen each other for almost a month.

Our original plan had been only blackmail. But again the question of danger arose. How long could I blackmail you and get away with it?

And so we determined to strike once and get *all* of your money. . .

At the moment you are reading this, Diana and I are increasing the distance between you and us. The world is a large place, Mr. Reeves, and I do not think you will find us. Not without a time machine.

And how did I manage that time machine?

It was an elaborate hoax, Mr. Reeves, but with two hundred and fifty thousand dollars at stake, one can afford to be elaborate.

When you left me alone with my time machine ten days ago, Mr. Reeves, I turned on two devices concealed above the room. One created noise and the other created wind.

And then I quickly *folded* the time machine.

You have no doubt by now noticed that it is extremely light. And if you will look again, you will discover that there are a number of concealed hinges which allow one to fold it into a compact shape.

Then I removed the grate of one of the "ventilators," pushed the collapsed machine through into the small cubicle behind the wall, followed into the cubicle myself, and pulled the grating back into place behind me.

I watched as you re-entered the room, Mr. Reeves, and I allowed you only thirty seconds of astonishment before I turned on the noise and wind machines again. I did not want you to collect your wits and examine the room.

When you left, I simply crawled out of my hiding place and unfolded my machine.

I think that was rather ingenious, don't you?

But you say that is impossible? There *is* no hiding place for the time machine—even folded—and for me?

The room is absolutely solid? You have examined it yourself and you would stake your life on it?

You are right, Mr. Reeves. There is no hiding place here. The room *is* solid.

But you see, Mr. Reeves, there are *two* garages.

The first one, to which I took you blindfolded, is in reality located several miles from here. It is the same type of building—a standard brand erected by the thousands in this area—and I took great pains to make it an exact duplicate of the one you are in now—even to the position of the tools lying on the bench, the ladder against the wall.

The two garages are identical—with some exceptions. The time machine room in one of them is slightly smaller—to allow for the hiding place—and the noise and wind machines are installed under the eaves. As for the ventilators, with the exception of the one I used to enter my hiding place, they are actually blowers.

After I drove you back to your apartment, I returned, packed my time machine, took the license plates off the wall, and brought them here.

Those license plates?

You are a clever man, Mr. Reeves. I grant that and I have taken advantage of that cleverness. I nailed them to a conspicuous place on the wall with the express hope that you would utilize them to track me down—but to *this* place.

I wanted you to examine this garage. I wanted you to be absolutely satisfied that the time machine had to be genuine. I was in a neighboring lot watching you after I had turned out the house lights.

I am, of course, not Henry Pruitt. The license plates belonged to the former tenant of the house.

Nevertheless, for the purposes of this letter, I remain, most gratefully,

Your servant,

Henry Pruitt.

I tore the letter to bits and snatched a peen hammer from the workbench.

As I smashed the time machine to smithereens, I couldn't help the horrible thought that perhaps someone, in a real time machine, might at that very moment be in the room watching me.

And laughing.

Checklist of the Cardula Stories

"Kid Cardula," *Alfred Hitchcock's Mystery Magazine* June 1976

"The Cardula Detective Agency" *Alfred Hitchcock's Mystery Magazine* March 1977

"The Canvas Caper" *Alfred Hitchcock's Mystery Magazine* August 1977

"Cardula to the Rescue" *Alfred Hitchcock's Mystery Magazine* December   1977

"Cardula and the Kleptomaniac" *Alfred Hitchcock's Mystery Magazine* April 1978

"Cardula's Revenge " *Alfred Hitchcock's Mystery Magazine* November 1978

"The Return of Cardula" *Alfred Hitchcock's Mystery Magazine* February 3 1982

"Cardula and the Locked Rooms" *Alfred Hitchcock's Mystery Magazine* March 31 1982

"Cardula and the Briefcase" *Mike Shayne Mystery Magazine* June 1983

"Upside Down World.", *Alfred Hitchcock Mystery Magazine* May 1962
- Behind the Locked Door, *Four Square,* 1967

"Pearls Before Wine." *Mike Shayne Mystery Magazine* August 1968

"Swing High." *Alfred Hitchcock's Mystery Magazine* May 1965

"Play a Game of Cyanide." Alfred Hitchcock's Mystery Magazine May 1961

"Box in a Box." *Alfred Hitchcock's Mystery Magazine* October 1977

"The Crime Machine." *Alfred Hitchcock's Mystery Magazine* January 1961

Cardula and the Locked Rooms

Cardula and the Locked Rooms by Jack Ritchie is printed on 60-pound paper, and is designed by Jeffrey Marks using InDesign. The type is Garamond, a group of fonts named for French engraver Claude Garamond. The cover is by Joshua Luboski. The first edition was published in a perfect-bound softcover edition and a clothbound edition. *Cardula and the Locked Room* was printed and bound by Imprint Press. The book was published in January 2026 by Crippen & Landru Publishers.

Crippen & Landru, Publishers
P. O. Box 532057
Cincinnati, OH 45253
Web: www.Crippenlandru.com
E-mail: info@crippenlandru.com

Since 1994, Crippen & Landru has published more than 100 first editions of short-story collections by important detective and mystery writers.

This is the best edited, most attractively packaged line of mystery books introduced in this decade. The books are equally valuable to collectors and readers. [Mystery Scene Magazine]

The specialty publisher with the most star-studded list is Crippen & Landru, which has produced short story collections by some of the biggest names in contemporary crime fiction. [Ellery Queen's Mystery Magazine]

God bless Crippen & Landru. [The Strand Magazine]

A monument in the making is appearing year by year from Crippen & Landru, a small press devoted exclusively to publishing the criminous short story. [Alfred Hitchcock's Mystery Magazine]

Crippen & Landru
Lost Classics

Peter Godfrey. *The Newtonian Egg.* 2002.

Craig Rice. *Murder, Mystery, and Malone.* 2002 eBook, $8.99

Charles B. Child. *The Sleuth of Baghdad.* 2002.

Stuart Palmer. *Hildegarde Withers, Uncollected Riddles.* 2002 eBook $8.99

Christianna Brand. *The Spotted Cat.* 2002

Raoul Whitfield. *Jo Gar's Casebook.* 2002.

William Campbell Gault. *Marksman.* 2003.

Gerald Kersh. *Karmesin.* 2003 eBook, $8.99

C. Daly King. *The Complete Curious Mr. Tarrant.* 2003 eBook $8.99

Helen McCloy. *The Pleasant Assassin.* 2003

William DeAndrea. *Murder – All Kinds.* 2003

Anthony Berkeley. *The Avenging Chance.* 2004

Joseph Commings. *Banner Deadlines.* 2004 eBook $8.99

Erle Stanley Gardner. *The Danger Zone.* 2004 eBook $8.99

T. S. Stribling. *Dr. Poggioli: Criminologist.* 2004 eBook $8.99

Margaret Millar. *The Couple Next Door.* 2004

Gladys Mitchell. *Sleuth's Alchemy.* 2005

Philip Warne/Howard Macy. *Who Was Guilty?* 2005 eBook $8.99

Dennis Lynds writing as Michael Collins. *Slot-Machine Kelly.* 2005

Julian Symons. *The Detections of Francis Quarles.* 2006

Rafael Sabatini. *The Evidence of the Sword.* 2006 eBook, $8.99

Erle Stanley Gardner. *The Casebook of Sidney Zoom.* 2006, eBook $8.99

Ellis Peters. *The Trinity Cat.* 2006

Lloyd Biggle. *The Grandfather Rastin Mysteries.* 2007

Max Brand. *Masquerade.* 2007

Mignon Eberhart. *Dead Yesterday.* 2007

Hugh Pentecost. *The Battles of Jericho.* 2008

Victor Canning. *The Minerva Club.* 2009

Anthony Boucher and Denis Green. *The Casebook of Gregory Hood.* 2009

Vera Caspary. *The Murder in the Stork Club.* 2009

Michael Innes. *Appleby Talks About Crime.* 2010

Phillip Wylie. *Ten Thousand Blunt Instruments*. 2010

Erle Stanley Gardner. *The Exploits of the Patent Leather Kid.* 2010, eBook, $8.99

Vincent Cornier. *The Duel of Shadows.* 2011, eBook, $8.99

E. X. Ferrars. *The Casebook of Jonas P. Jonas.* 2012

Charlotte Armstrong. *Night Call.* 2014, eBook, $8.99

Phyllis Bentley. *Chain of Witnesses.* 2014

Patrick Quentin. *The Puzzles of Peter Duluth.* 2016, Clothbound $29, eBook $8.99

Frederick Irving Anderson . *The Purple Flame.* 2016, Clothbound $29, Trade Paperback $19

Anthony Gilbert. *Sequel to Murder.* 2017, Clothbound $29

James Holding. *The Zanzibar Shirt Mystery.* 2018, Clothbound $29

William Brittain. *The Man Who Read Mysteries.* 2018, Clothbound $32, Trade Paperback $1922 eBook $8.99

Q. Patrick. *The Cases of Lieutenant Trant.* 2019

Erle Stanley Gardner. *Hot Cash, Cold Clews.* 2020, Clothbound $32, Trade Paperback $22, eBook $8.99

Freeman Wills Crofts, *The 9.50 Up Express.* 2021, Clothbound $32, Trade Paperback $22, eBook $8.99

Stuart Palmer. *Hildegarde Withers, Final Riddles?* 2021, Clothbound $32, Trade Paperback $22, eBook $8.99

Patrick Quentin. *Hunt in the Dark.* 2021

William Brittain. *The Man Who Solved Mysteries.* 2022, Clothbound $32, Trade Paperback $1922 eBook $8.99

John Creasey. *Gideon and the Young Toughs.* 2022, Clothbound $35, Trade Paperback $20, eBook $8.99

Pierre Very. *The Secret of the Pointed Tower.* 2023, Clothbound $32, Trade Paperback $20

Anthony Berkeley. *The Avenging Chance and Even More Stories (Enlarged with Two Stories).* 2023, Trade Paperback $19, eBook

Richard and Francis Lockridge. *Flair for Murder.* 2024, Clothbound $32, Trade Paperback $22

White, Ethel Lina. *Blackout and Other Stories of Suspense.* 2025, Clothbound $35, Trade Paperback $22

Van Dine, S.S. The Almost Perfect Crime. 2025, Clothbound $35, Trade Paperback $22

Subscriptions

Subscribers agree to purchase each forthcoming publication, either the Regular Series or the Lost Classics or (preferably) both. Collectors can thereby guarantee receiving limited editions, and readers won't miss any favorite stories.

Subscribers receive a discount of 20% off the list price (and the same discount on our backlist) and a specially commissioned short story by a major writer in a deluxe edition as a gift at the end of the year.

The point for us is that, since customers don't pick and choose which books they want, we have a guaranteed sale even before the book is published, and that allows us to be more imaginative in choosing short story collections to issue.

That's worth the 20% discount for us. Sign up now and start saving. Email us at orders@crippenlandru.com or visit our website at www.crippenlandru.com on our subscription page.